ROMANCE IN VALIANT BOOK THREE

GLITTER AND THE GROUCH

MARY PAT JOHNS

Scrivenings PRESS

Quench your thirst for story.

www.ScriveningsPress.com

Published by Scrivenings Press LLC
15 Lucky Lane
Morrilton, Arkansas 72110
https://ScriveningsPress.com

Printed in the United States of America

Paperback ISBN 978-1-64917-416-1
eBook ISBN 978-1-64917-417-8

Editors: Regina Rudd Merrick and Heidi Glick

Cover by Linda Fulkerson, www.bookmarketinggraphics.com

All characters are fictional, and any resemblance to real people, either factual or historical, is purely coincidental.

I really enjoyed this book from the very first chapter. Rory and Vi both have some baggage from their past. I loved reading how they both grew closer to one another during the remodeling process. They sure had some struggles to deal with, like squatters, fire, and more, but they really came together to get through those times. I also LOVED that they sought God through the trials of both the remodel and the "baggage" of their past. I HIGHLY recommend this book to anyone who enjoys the Christian Romance genre! I am very much looking forward to future books in this series! WONDERFUL BOOK!

KENDRA NEAL, REVIEWER

Don't let the cover fool you into thinking that this is going to be just a lighthearted romance ... because this story truly is so much more than that. Both Rory and Vi are characters who have had difficult pasts that they are still healing from in many ways. I appreciate that the author isn't afraid to take on difficult topics, but does so with grace and sensitivity, keeping it realistic, but also not too heavy. If you are looking for a beautifully written Christian romance with genuine and imperfect characters, this is absolutely one you won't want to miss.

RANDI SAMPSON, REVIEWER

*This book is dedicated to the many competitors and organizers who
have helped make the Texas Water Safari what it is.
If we don't have goals that stretch beyond our self-imposed limits,
how will we ever know what we're capable of?*

CHAPTER ONE

"Easy now, Mrs. Metzler. This isn't a race." Natalie Jacobs kept a watchful eye on the small, frail woman as she sat on a workout bench, hefting a five-pound disc back and forth against her chest. "Keep the pace slow and even. Building strength doesn't happen fast. It happens with consistency."

"Call me Tillie. I'm going to be late for my hair appointment. Besides, my *physical therapist*"—she stressed the term as if Nat wouldn't know anything about it— "said arm exercises aren't important. *He* said they're boring and unnecessary." She looked into the wall mirror. Frowning, she patted at her snowy white hair.

Nat snugged the clipboard under her arm, stifling a grin. Tillie's PT had said no such thing. Silas Tarkington had told Nat to make sure the woman didn't shirk or miscount on the more challenging exercises.

"Slow and even." She kept her voice upbeat. "If you wear yourself out, you won't want to come back. And I would miss you terribly." A corner of Nat's mouth tugged upward, though she found it increasingly hard to stay on task.

Tillie snorted as she started up again, slowing her movements a nano-fraction.

Glancing around the large workout area, Nat's mind absently registered a barrel-chested man with tattoo sleeves on both arms, heaving dumbbells in a biceps exercise. Peeps' Gym pumped with the energy of people working out. Athletes ran on treadmills. Other members walked with buddies on the circular track. The muffled noise of weights clanking and the ever-present scent of antiseptic completed the active environment.

Nat couldn't imagine working anywhere else. In the short time she'd been employed here, Peeps had become the premier exercise facility in Valiant, Texas. No other gym matched its offerings or popularity.

"Did you count the reps?" Nat's attention traveled back to her client, who had stopped her slight movement to stare at Tattoo Guy. Tillie gave a noncommittal shrug. Nat pressed, "Close to fifteen?"

"Whatever you say, sweet cheeks." The elderly woman set the disc on the end of the workout bench. "What I want to know is if you have a boyfriend." Her made-up eyes had a decidedly wicked gleam.

The polite smile Nat pasted on warred with the answer that popped into her mind. "How about doing another set?"

Tillie cackled but didn't pick up the disc. "Seems to me a pretty girl like you, what with the wavy hair, flashy eyes, and your slim figure, would have them comin' around all the time."

The sigh Nat had been holding in escaped like a convict on the lam. Getting any actual work out of the woman was akin to pushing an elephant up a flight of stairs. Mr. Every-Single-Rep-Counts Tarkington, Peeps' in-house physical therapist, knew it too, or else he wouldn't have stressed the whole keep-an-eye-on-her bit. Yet, if Nat told him the truth, since he would inevitably ask, he'd act as if it was her fault Tillie wasn't more motivated.

Good thing Nat had a plan to distract him.

"C'mon, Tillie." Nat's pleasant façade slipped as an edge of steel entered her tone. "Show me what those arms can do."

"'Bout time you kicked in. Girl, you got a feisty tiger locked up inside." Tillie winked at her, then picked up the disc and energetically pumped.

Nat's lips twitched into a smile. All Tillie had wanted was a genuine reaction. To be seen instead of simply being handled. Nat could relate.

THE ABSOLUTE PERFECT OPPORTUNITY. Silas's Army-issue gym bag rested on the bench next to the wall. Nat cupped a hand over her mouth to keep from crowing. Noise drifted from Peeps' physical therapy room. She peeked through the large see-through window, momentarily mesmerized by the sight of Silas working with a toddler. He kneeled with his arms out, his lips stretched into a gentle smile.

Does it hurt?

"Walk to me, Emily. Walk." His words carried a sing-song inflection, another first to Nat's ears. Silas came across as a man of few words. To her, anyway. Which only made Nat more determined to garner a reaction. The silken-haired little blonde took another unsteady step toward him on the pseudo-wood floor. He widened his eyes, intentionally dropping his mouth open. "See what you did, Em? Come to me." Leaning forward, he beckoned her with his hands.

Spellbound, Nat gazed at the two, then she remembered why she came.

Emily took one more step, pulling her hands out of her

mom's, and fell into Silas's embrace. The baby laid her head on his shoulder as he massaged her back. Snuggling her close, he murmured something in her ear. Nat's arms tingled. She stepped back, shifting away from the sweet scene. The tender display nettled her. Silas had always acted cool, even aloof, to her. During their paddling runs, and more lately, the pranks, he kept his distance. Similar to dealing with a taciturn lump of … whatever. Nope. Not going there. She wasn't a toddler or a client in need of anything the man offered.

"Aww. Look at her, Silas. She feels safe with you," Emily's mom cooed.

Despite the note to self, Nat blinked the moisture from her eyes. She peeked inside the PT room. Silas was still holding Emily, engrossed in a conversation with the baby's mom. She looked at her phone, then they peered at his laptop.

Nat dug into her carryall and pulled out a small container. She unzipped Silas's bag, carefully opened the container, then poured the contents inside. She shook the bag with vigor and zipped it shut. There. That ought to keep him occupied for a while. Too busy to get on her case about Tillie. Quickly, she stuffed the container back in her tote. Silas's voice swept closer.

"Walk Emily everywhere, Mrs. Klimas. The more you require her to walk, the faster she'll do it on her own."

They paused in the doorway. "I do, but everything takes twice as long," the young mother said, on the verge of a whine. "She's good about walking for you. With me, she scoots around on her bottom because it's faster."

Nat stole back the way she came, certain Silas hadn't seen her.

SILAS CHUCKLED as Emily sucked her thumb in contentment. Kids understood far more than adults thought they did. This little one had already figured out Mom would capitulate. "Sounds entirely normal for any kid, especially one with low muscle tone. It takes patience, for sure. If you want results …"

He grinned, tracing a finger around Emily's earlobe. Her rosebud lips erupted into joyful baby giggles.

Giving her one last squeeze, he held her high, then flew her squishy little body like an airplane into her mother's arms. "Here you go."

If only the rest of his clients were as engaging as this little sweetheart. The way her lower lip stuck out when she didn't want to cooperate lightened his day. He stifled a sigh. Three more weeks with her, then they'd move on.

Once they'd left, he made notes about the appointment on his laptop, then glanced at the clock. Enough time between clients to squeeze in a workout if he hurried. His gym bag stayed on the outside bench for quick getaways. The relentless ringing of the office phone posed another problem. He'd had no choice except to depend on voicemail, though it ranked low on his list of options. Hopefully, the issue would be resolved soon enough. The new position Silas had applied for came with a receptionist.

Grabbing his bag off the bench, he strode into the Peeps' lobby. Briefly, he wondered what Nat wanted. He'd spied her ponytail through the picture window. She'd disappeared by the time he looked again.

The change from active military duty to civilian life had been tough. Working at this first-class gym complex had eased the transition. It had given him something to do while he decided on his next step. As he'd prayed about it over the months, the answer had been deceptively simple—a career at

Peeps would fill his cup to the brim. Peeps had become the place where he helped people. A stable environment, compared to his early childhood and sniper missions. The idea of starting over somewhere else had no appeal. He wanted what he'd achieved here. No other gym in Valiant supplied the elements he needed. Peace. Order. An obsessive bent toward cleanliness. Even if his brain insisted he'd overlooked something equally essential.

Extra sets on the resistance machines would decimate his gnawing need for more. He refused to give a shred of mind space to what exactly "more" meant.

The whir of a vacuum greeted him in the men's dressing room. Silas stepped over the snaky cord, plunked his bag on a bench next to a row of lockers, and unzipped it. He stared uncomprehendingly into his gym bag as silver bits flurried into the air. All over the clean clothes in his bag, all over the floor, all over him. He reached a hand into the shimmery dust to pull out his T-shirt. Glitter cascaded everywhere. Fierce knowledge split through his bedazzled mind.

Nat!

Now he knew why his infuriating co-worker had been lurking outside the physical therapy room. He sifted through the bag, hoping the omnipresent silver hadn't penetrated to the bottom. It had. He raked a hand through his hair, realizing too late he'd streaked glitter through it. Silas hated a mess. His skin prickled with the stuff. He impatiently swiped at the streak on his arm. The glitter multiplied beyond dirt or sand. It blew past his ability to deal with it rationally. He took a deep breath, exhaling in a slow stream, willing himself to calm down.

Yeah, Nat was easy on the eyes. Yeah, he might have pranked her once or twice. This time, however, she'd gone too far. A small inner voice reminded him she couldn't have known about his aversion to messes—even shiny silvery ones. A confetti shower wouldn't bother her one whit. Frivolous. Unencumbered with consequences. She'd pay for this devilry.

He breathed words long stashed away as unfitting to his renewed commitment to Christ. He yanked the glittery shirt from his gym bag. Jamming his service cap on his head, he marched out of the Peeps' dressing room.

His mission in life boiled down to one slender thread. Find the woman who'd invaded his space.

NAT STOOD AT THE PEEPS' deli counter, allowing a large swallow of green smoothie to slide down her parched throat. Mm. She tasted more peanut butter than anything else, but the green color gave evidence to the yummy kale nutrients. She held the slender plastic cup toward the deli server with a nod. Perfect. She rubbed her aching neck. Past time for a massage. Her early workout had been vicious.

Coasting on physical activity for the rest of the day suited her fine. That left two clients, then paperwork from the self-defense seminar she'd conducted over the weekend. Once she ticked those items off her to-do list, she'd pester Jesse for a peek at the blueprints for the upcoming rehab facility. So far, his only concession had been to call her Nosy. Oh, well. She'd gleaned her prying techniques from Rory, his best friend. Jesse would relent, eventually. All the years she'd tagged after them were paying off. Mellow chatter from workout members filled the air. A contented sigh slipped before she drank more smoothie.

As much as she enjoyed the interaction with her clients, her satisfaction as a personal trainer had waned. Nat could pinpoint the exact moment her attention had shifted. It happened when her brother Jesse, Director of Operations for Peeps, mentioned the position of business CEO had opened for the rehab wing.

Since her official graduation last spring with a degree in business administration, her new goal was to prove she could manage Peeps' new facility. She'd been over the moon when Jesse suggested she fill out an application. As much as she hated to admit it, she was counting on him to teach her how to be a top-notch business administrator. She'd checked around town. No other gym director possessed a fraction of his management skill.

After a glance at her fitness watch, she peered into the lobby. She'd best scoot before Silas showed up. Her nose wrinkled with pleasure when she remembered his gym bag. Best prank ever.

Not that she paid much attention to Silas, aside from a growing curiosity about what made him tick. He'd salted her egg whites the day before, knowing full well she never used salt. So, maybe she'd been too outspoken about her nutritional habits. Or because she'd put sugar in his coffee last week. The man defined uptight. She'd thoroughly enjoyed the way his normally unreadable eyes had glowed.

Inhaling the sweet smell of banana, she picked up her pace, only to find her forward motion halted by iron band biceps wrapping around her, holding her in place.

Silas. His fresh soap scent wafted into her senses. Much too close to her ear, he whispered, "Gotcha, Pranky."

Only then did she realize he was swishing the sabotaged T-shirt across her back with one hand. She squeezed around to face him. The uncomfortable feeling of glitter scratched her arms. As the T-shirt moved toward her hair, she struggled, losing her smoothie. The cup's hard plastic snapped, causing icy liquid to saturate her shirt. Satisfaction registered in a small part of her brain at Silas's wrinkled brow as her smoothie drenched the front of his T-shirt. The rest of the ill-fated drink spread with the speed of a fast-flowing river on the white tile.

A momentary hush fell as onlookers stared, then laughter erupted. Until an itty-bitty guy toddled over, lost his balance, and fell in the green goo. Nat thrust her arms out, attempting to intercept him before he hit the floor. Too late. His backside smacked the tile with a thud. She winced as he caught his breath. The ensuing squall proved more suitable to a barnyard than the Peeps' deli.

Nat kneeled next to him, wiping his arm with her used napkin. He only howled louder and jerked away. His mother pushed her aside to console him.

The laughter had changed to looks of disapproval as people cut a wide swathe around the mess. She rose shakily to her feet. Silas was sludging smoothie with his bare hands from the tile into a cup. Glitter trailed down his cheeks and into a corner of his lip. The T-shirt lay on the floor, an unrecognizable blob. She grabbed it to soak the liquid dripping off the counter. Each swipe left a silver streak. Her hands sparkled. She could only imagine what her face and hair looked like.

Emilio, the maintenance man, headed her direction with a mop and bucket. The child's cries had softened into muffled sobs. A familiar-looking man in a business suit talked to the toddler's mother. After a terse conversation, he handed her a business card, then pointed to the main reception desk. Nat stood rooted to the spot. She should know him, but names often eluded her.

The child's mother favored her with a scowl as she made her way out of the deli. Even the toddler cast her an accusing look.

Before she could move, Suit Guy stood in front of her. Silas quickly rose from where he kneeled on the floor. Nat couldn't shake the notion they had both crossed an irretrievable line.

Eyebrows arching into the heavens, the silver-haired man glowered as he gazed at their lanyards. His air of authority clobbered her with recognition.

Oh, no.

Jesse called this man Big Gun, but never to his face. As in head honcho. The alpha and omega of all things Peeps-related.

Breaking the awkward silence, Silas spoke grimly. "I apologize, sir. This was my fault."

Mr. Spence's eyes narrowed as he observed the patch on Silas's cap. "Of all people, *vet*, you should know better than to pull a stunt like this."

CHAPTER TWO

"What made you think this prank was a good idea, Nat?" Jesse's dark eyes sparked with irritation. "The part where you poured glitter into Silas's gym bag or when you lost control of your smoothie." Outrage spiked his words.

"The smoothie part was an accident—" she protested, then clamped her mouth shut. Explaining how Silas's proximity had squeezed it out of her hand wouldn't help their case.

Shortly after the fiasco in the deli, she'd barely had time to change her shirt before she'd received a text from Jesse. Obviously, Silas had received a summons too. Now they sat in his office like two recalcitrant school kids.

She gazed at the picture of her and Jesse on his bookshelf, the only decorative item in the small room. The photo, nestled amid stacks of manuals on how to run Peeps, reminded her of when she'd had her handsome brother all to herself. They'd been close, not counting today. Nat had given him the photo to help ward off forward females.

At one time, they were together so much, people often concluded they were a couple. Before he'd fallen head over heels in love with Brenna, his accountant. Nat liked Brenna. The sweet-natured woman classified as the perfect match for her competitive brother. Since their engagement, though, he hung out with her all the time, leaving Nat to herself more often than not. Nat pushed the prick of jealousy away and tuned back in to Jesse's clipped speech.

"And you." Jesse's hot gaze landed on Silas, who was making a career out of staring at the floor. "Since when do paybacks ever happen on the job? Or at all, despite the provocation?"

The sharp comeback on the tip of Nat's tongue melted into something more palatable. "It was my fault, Jess. I started it." She caught a whiff of her hair. Ugh. It'd be a while before she could stomach peanut butter again.

For the first time since they entered the room, Silas spoke. "No, I'm to blame. If I'd let it go, nothing else would have happened."

Nat doubted that. She would have made something else happen even if he'd ignored the glitter prank. Once on a roll, she rarely stopped until she'd gained her goal—or in this case, desired reaction. Hence the mess they were in.

Her voice thready with fear, she asked, "Have we lost our jobs?" This couldn't be happening. One dumb prank and her future at Peeps was in jeopardy. A future she desperately wanted. She cast a side eye at Silas. The beaded sweat on his forehead betrayed his nervousness. The stoicism he wore like a badge had vanished. Because of her foolish actions, his future was also in peril.

Jesse tossed his pen onto the desk and plopped back in his chair. Exasperation thinned his lips. "You certainly should have." He let those awful words dangle until they both squirmed. "Mr. Spence barreled in here, spitting fire. He wanted me to sack both of you. Fortunately, his quick response to the baby—*a baby*—falling on the slippery floor you created," his voice rose with each jab of his finger, "probably saved us a lawsuit."

"How much?" Silas asked.

"What?" Confusion colored Nat's understanding.

"How much did his quick response cost Peeps?

Cost? She bit her lip. Why did it always come down to money? It hadn't crossed her mind this shenanigan would cause a payout.

"Three months of free membership with childcare fees." Jesse looked at them. "It's coming out of your paychecks."

Nat hung her head. Ramen noodles for the next month she could handle. Still, she couldn't bring herself to ask the most important thing again.

Her reticence didn't affect Silas. "What about our jobs?"

THE GLARE JESSE shot him pressed on Silas's last nerve. Still, he needed to know. He swallowed hard. They both deserved the boot for the way they'd acted. Sheer stupidity. Only he didn't want Nat to suffer for his lapse. They both got caught up in the prank … and forgot they were at work.

For Pete's sake, he'd survived a war zone. Been shot at more times than he remembered. Taken lives in the line of duty. Talk about a lapse in judgment. He'd chased a woman down and rubbed her with a shiny shirt. Over this, he would lose his future?

The only future he cared about. He couldn't move to another city. Gramps and Petey needed him. Silas wouldn't leave them again.

"Your jobs still hang in the balance. However, with some fast-talking, I finagled a second chance for both of you—*if* you'll quit acting like juveniles long enough to take it." Jesse's grim tone should have been a warning. However, the reference to a second chance piqued Silas's interest.

"What are the terms?" Nat asked. Good. She sounded engaged. He swallowed the huff rising in his throat. She possessed great skill for flying off to Never Never Land. Whether she could stay the course when things got tough remained unknown.

The crease in Jesse's forehead deepened. "You're both serious paddlers, right? I mean, it's how this 'friendly rivalry' got started."

Silas cut a side look at Nat's guilt-ridden face. Jesse couldn't have known about the "friendly rivalry" unless she'd blabbed it. She glared back at him in challenge.

"So here's what I proposed to Mr. Spence," Jesse said. "You guys are in the running for executive positions once the new rehab wing goes up." The last words turned hard as chips as he motioned to Nat. "You are a strong contender for business CEO." His thumb and forefinger pointed gun-style at Silas's chest. "You're slated to head up the actual rehab." He appeared to be considering his words. "Mr. Spence was horrified over your lack of professional behavior. He wants to make sure you two can hold it together for Peeps' sake. You need to show beyond any doubt you're committed to cooperation—for the long haul."

Silas and Nat exchanged uneasy looks. What did this have to do with canoe racing?

"To that end, I suggested you two put your paddling skills to work. Prove you'll do anything necessary to get the job done."

Jesse continued, as if his communication made perfect sense. *Far from it.* "The Texas Water Safari is right around the corner. You both excelled at the prelim. Now you're doing practice runs for the big race. Am I right?"

Nat's head bobbed with eagerness. For a moment, Silas wished he had an ounce of her passion. They had been training for the TWS for months, each doing their solo runs. Whenever they spied each other on the river, it became a competition to see who would finish first.

Silas waited warily. He sensed a trap.

"In order to keep your jobs *and* stay in the running for future promotions, you're gonna have to change your focus. Mr. Spence wants you to enter and finish the TWS together." The hard grooves on Jesse's forehead eased as his gaze settled on Nat. Boss or not, he adored her. Rumor had it he'd instigated a fight because her boyfriend treated her shabbily.

The look Jesse gave Silas reinforced his musings. Only ... the man couldn't have said what Silas heard.

"It's all good, Jess," Nat chirped far too cheerily.

Jesse cracked his knuckles, a sure sign of impatience. "Competing as one unit, bug."

The brotherly term of endearment didn't help. Nat's face reflected Silas's conflicting emotions. Stunned into a one-syllable answer, she whispered, "Oh."

Silas spoke past the ever-growing lump in his throat. "Jesse, we've been training solo for months. I'm not sure you understand what you're asking. A twosome is a whole different deal ..."

Jesse regarded him with a mix of steel and compassion. "I understand, but I'm not asking."

"That's not fair! Silas is a serious contender in the solo event. He could win it. You can't do this ... I've never ... we can't ..." Nat's protests shut down at Jesse's stern countenance.

Fierce river rapids had nothing on Silas's churning stomach.

Even if Nat's silver-tongued brother convinced her to go along with his terrible idea, Silas wouldn't agree. His time on the river had become sacred. There, he could forget the past. Recharge his ever-waning spiritual battery. Soak in the goodness of God. He'd never have a moment's peace in the same boat with Nat for two-hundred and sixty miles. Jesse had just prescribed nuclear war. It wouldn't come to physical blows, but words were terrible weapons. Nat talked too much. It sliced through him like cheese in a grater.

CHAPTER THREE

Silas hustled away from the meeting to gain distance from Nat. Except she'd followed him down the hall. *Pest.* He inhaled another breath of the fresh smell of carpet cleaner, ignoring her calls for him to stop.

Despite his extended strides, she closed the gap between them, putting a hand on his shoulder. "We have to talk," she said breathlessly.

Even as he shrugged her hand off, his steps slowed. "I have an appointment."

"We have to discuss the boat race."

"It's not going anywhere."

"It is for us. We've got to figure out what to do."

He stopped, staring at her. "There's no 'we' to it. I'm looking for a new job."

"You don't mean it." Impatience underscored her words. "You don't want to leave Peeps any more than I do. I'd rather suck up to this silly scheme of theirs than lose my future here. It's your future too. You have to do this with me."

Silas's shoulders slumped. She nailed it, however much it

pinched. Irritation hardly described his feelings about the situation they'd gotten themselves in. The fiasco in the deli had torpedoed their chances with Mr. Spence. Fixing the awful impression they'd made ranked paramount, of course. But using the canoe race to do it seemed bizarre ... meddlesome. The infringement on his personal life stung. He valued his solitary time in the boat. A partner would strip him bare—open to scrutiny. No way he would ever do that again.

"Don't you want to be in charge of the new rehab?"

More than anything.

The plea in Nat's light brown eyes frayed his chaotic emotions. Finally, he said, "We can talk." The only concession he would make at the moment.

Nat's blinding smile nearly undid him. "Good! I'll text you when and where."

She's as bossy as her brother, minus the title. Pivoting back toward the PT rooms, he grunted noncommittally. He had nothing else to give until he could get ... un-frustrated with the whole situation.

As if *un-frustrated* would ever happen around Nat. The woman irked him to the core.

THE SAME EVENING, Nat walked into the garage where Silas had his homemade paddling system set up. He'd refused to meet her for dinner or any other place she suggested. When she wouldn't give up, he'd consented to letting her come to his place. If his shabby digs and sweaty workout clothes disgusted her, all the better. She could leave or go play with the cats Vi had coaxed him into keeping.

Vi. Much as Silas had enjoyed the petite redhead's company, he'd never had a chance. Not with the way she looked at Rory. So in the time-honored, male tradition, Silas made the most of any opportunity to aggravate the guy. Hard to resist, since he was everything Silas wasn't. Charming. Successful. A face women flocked to, even if he acted like a hot mess around Vi.

Funny thing was, Silas wasn't upset that Rory got the girl. It seemed inevitable and only confirmed what Silas knew from the beginning. Those two were meant for each other. Who was he to begrudge their happiness? No matter that his end of the deal turned into a nasty dog bite while protecting Vi, and more cats than he knew what to do with. He tried not to picture how cute Nat would look with one of his felines snuggled next to her face.

Silas pushed the irritating thought away. He waved Nat in, disgruntled she'd actually showed up. He'd been hoping she wouldn't. After a quick glance around the tools neatly suspended on the pegboard he'd hung, her eyes landed on his homemade workout gear.

"Impressive." A single blade paddle had a wire cable attached to it just above the blade. The cable stretched, then threaded through a rotating pulley attached to the roof next to the garage doors. The cable wire attached to a five-gallon bucket on the cement floor. He added or subtracted weights to adjust the cable tension.

"You want to try it?" Silas offered, expecting her to chicken out.

"Yes!"

Of course, Nat wouldn't back down. He let the paddle dangle, adjusting the weight in the bucket while she got situated. The temptation to pile the weight on tugged at him, but the desire to see her true capacity won out.

"Okay. Show me your technique. I'll count your stroke rate."

She nodded. Both of her hands were already on the paddle, warming up. "I'll give it my best shot." She paddled hard on one side. After seven strokes, she switched to the other side.

Once her strokes shallowed, Silas coached her. His heart rate sped up as he instructed her how to increase the paddle stroke rate and when to switch sides. Nat giving her best made it hard to keep his distance.

After fifteen minutes, he yelled, *stop*. To her credit, she hadn't given up, though her paddle had slowed. Nowhere near enough strength to reclaim her starting pace. Or keep up with him.

Nat rose slowly from the chair, carefully wrapping her arms around her middle. Rivulets of sweat ran from her temples to her jaws. She gave him a cheeky grin. "Got a way to go. Sweet workout though."

Silas regarded her in a new light. Possibly admiration. "You have to maintain a consistent stroke rate—fifty-five to sixty strokes a minute—for the entire race, to compete."

Her lips scooched to one side. "I'm nowhere close. I get it. From what I understand about the TWS, winning is a stretch for first-timers."

"It matters to me," Silas retorted.

Her large brown eyes regarded him with a mix of determination and sympathy. "We're in this together now with a different goal. Nothing's changed since you told me you want the rehab position, right?"

He stared at her, refusing to answer. She knew perfectly well nothing had changed.

She continued with a smoothness he couldn't help but envy. Ongoing communication made him want to bite his tongue in half. "So our new goal is to set aside what we want *now* in order to gain what we want *most*—our future with Peeps."

Nat's ability to parse a thorny issue down to a single thread terrified him.

He wanted no part of her glib tongue or a twosome ride down the river.

But it wouldn't hurt to listen.

"THE FIRST PROBLEM we have to tackle is the boat. Got any suggestions?" Nat frowned. Silas watched her lean gingerly against the outer garage wall. The soreness from her stroke workout was settling in.

"We'll check with Gramps first. He competed for years and has a boat shed." Silas didn't know why he volunteered the information. This twosome idea would never work.

Relief eased the knot between Nat's brows. "Here's hoping he has a boat we can use. If we can afford it."

"He won't charge us." A slight smile poked at his lips. "More likely, he'll want to tag along and tell stories."

A glint of mischief made Nat's eyes sparkle. "Sounds like fun. Maybe he'll give me the lowdown on you." Her lips screwed into a charming frown. "Have you thought about choosing the team captains?"

"I have someone in mind. Lacy is a nurse who's been coming in for therapy. We've kind of hit it off. I think she'll do a fine job." Too late, he realized how it sounded. In truth, they were fairly new acquaintances, though it wouldn't hurt if Nat thought otherwise. Her stiff posture portended an earful of opinion.

"The nurse part is okay. How do you know she'll go the distance? Team Captain isn't a cush job. I think Jesse should volunteer. He's the one who got us into this mess."

Silas shook his head. "Not Jesse."

"Why not Jesse?" Nat asked, spitfire lacing each word.

"Look, it's not about him being your brother—not entirely. Nat, you know how … intense he gets." Jesse's reaction to his sister's physical condition during a grueling canoe race wouldn't be pretty. "I'm just saying, let's think about it more."

Nat's hands landed on her hips. "I can handle Jesse. Most importantly, I trust him to be there for me. You need to think about your choice too." The look she gave him left no doubt what she thought of his "choice."

The race would be difficult enough without Jesse's glower at every checkpoint. "Have you talked to him about it?"

"No. Have you talked to Lacy?"

"No."

His brain cramped when Nat opened her mouth again. Her teeth were as straight as a row of pearls. "Good. We both have time. Next item on the agenda. We have to train. Learn how to sync our styles."

He cast her a dubious eye. "It's difficult."

"Thus, the reason we practice. Quit being such a Danny Downer." Exasperation filled her words.

"What was your solo strategy?" Silas doubted the analytical concept ever entered her flighty brain.

"I planned to follow in your draft. You know, stick as close to you as possible for as far down the river as possible."

"That was your plan?" Her honesty shocked him.

"Yes. I'm a novice. You're the participant I know the best. Now that we're in the same boat, I'll glean what you know. Even better."

He didn't know what worried him the most—her learning from him or the way her eyes sparkled like shiny river rocks.

CHAPTER FOUR

Silas stood in Gramps' RV storage-turned boat shed. Nat was supposed to meet him here to pick out a canoe. He hadn't told her he'd asked Lacy to join them.

Per her MO, Nat was late. He gave a mental eye roll. If their jobs and futures weren't at stake, he would not have agreed to do the race with Miss Fly-by-the-seat-of-her pants. A motor scooter in need of an oil change bleated outside the shed. The sputtering mimicked a dying goat.

Nat charged in, yanking off her helmet at the same time. The woman stayed in constant motion. Silas did a double-take as her dark hair spilled out of her helmet. The graceful shake of her head made it cascade down her back. Yep. Easy on the eyes. Too bad the rest of her came off so ... harum-scarum.

Canoes hung on both sides of the shed and on sawhorses in the middle. Gramps had been an avid canoe racer until the harsh conditions and physical stamina had made it too difficult to compete. Now he rented out canoes and watched the race with the same competitive zest.

"Nice stash of boats." Nat looked around the shed

appreciatively, directing her remark to Gramps, who had appeared with a gorgeous white retriever. The older man resembled the dog with his tangle of snowy hair.

"There's a story behind each one, little lady. They're like my kiddos." Silas's tension fled as he gazed at his grandpa, who beamed as if Nat had asked about his own flesh and blood.

"Gramps, this is Nat—we're, uh, considering a switch to tandem." He still couldn't bring himself to a full-on commitment. "Nat, my grandfather Bill."

Nat's attention had strayed. As usual. She kneeled to pet the dog. "What a gorgeous animal. What's his name?"

Gramps snorted. "Meet Elvis. People make over him so much, he forgets he's a dog. Have to say, it's odd to go tandem after the prelim. Official name for one male, one female category is mixed tandem unlimited."

"No argument with the odd part, Gramps." Silas didn't bother to keep the grouse out of his voice.

Nat's chin lifted. "It's a different challenge, that's all. If we each do our part."

This woman had the focus of a chigger. "I can handle my end, Glitter Girl."

Nat favored him with a smirk. "Grouch." She said it so softly, he involuntarily leaned closer to her. She turned to inspect the boats. "Any suggestions for our ride, Bill?"

Gramps smoothed white whiskers. "Depends on how you want to run it. I only got two tandems." He walked over to where Nat stood, pointing above their heads to a slender red canoe hanging from the metal ceiling. "There's one. Don't let her scruffy appearance fool ya. She's made of carbon fiber. Twenty feet long with a rudder." He measured them with a glance. "And narrow, which won't pose a problem for you two. The length makes her tippy, but she's fast."

He strode to the other side of the shed, kicking up powdery dirt. "The other is aluminum. Sturdy as they come. No rudder. The TWS is an unlimited race, which means no specs on the boat as long as it's powered by human muscle."

"You can use mine for free. If you look elsewhere, it'll cost anywhere from five-hundred to a thousand dollars per person. Whatever you two decide works for me," Gramps said.

Silas glanced at Nat. "We'll take the one with the rudder."

Nat shook her head vigorously. "Not so fast. I get a say."

"Why? I'll be the one steering."

Her brows raised. "Who says?"

"I'm heavier. More experienced."

"We started paddling about the same time. For what it's worth" Her glare could have torched him. "I'd rather have the rudder too. We'll trade off. I refuse to stare at the back of your head for four days."

"You think it's going to take four days? I'm planning on three."

"Things happen, Mr.-I-Got-This."

Silas opened his mouth with a sharp retort, but Gramps spoke up, his lazy drawl holding an edge of steel. "Toughest canoe race in the world. Best y'all get on the same page before the paddling starts."

"Oh, we will." Nat said breezily.

Silas nodded agreement. Eventually, she'd concede to his superior strength. It would make things much easier.

Gramps hadn't finished. "Tough enough to finish, much less place. If the bickering rides along, you'll slow to a crawl."

Conditions of the Texas Water Safari often proved so horrendous, most people considered the act of finishing a win in itself.

Even if he didn't agree with Gramps's assessment, seeing Nat blush made it all worth it.

He looked at Gramps. "We'll take the red one. Thank you for letting us use it rent-free."

Nat echoed her thanks, then walked around the boat as if searching for something. Yep. Attention of a ... Her eyes lit up at the hook on the bow end. Grinning, she pulled a small pink flag out of her pocket.

Silas peered at the wording. His eyes shot heavenward. "Really, Nat? Girl Power?" No way a flag with those words would fly from his boat.

"Yes. This ride needs some style. I'm all for celebrating girl power."

"Only I'm not a girl," he pointed out tartly.

Mischief shone from Nat's pecan-colored eyes. "Guess you'll have to bring your own flag, bubba."

He didn't miss the reference, however slight, to a country bumpkin. "Guess I don't need a flag to prove anything, Miss Girl Power."

Her brow winged upward. "You are tons of fun." She favored him with another grin, making sure he saw her lips form the word *grouch*.

"The flag's not part of it, Nat."

Her expression clearly communicated otherwise.

A distinctly feminine hello made them turn toward the street. Relief filled Silas, then consternation quickly took its place. A pretty woman with blue eyes and matching sundress appeared. "Oh, good. I'm in the right place." She walked over to Silas, hugging him as if they were a couple.

Silas cleared his throat, not at all certain how this would go. Nat was already in diva-mode.

"Hi, Lacy." He turned to Nat. "Nat, meet Lacy. She's come to hear what a team captain does."

TEAM CAPTAIN. What happened to thinking about it? Jesse had practically made them sign in blood that this would be a joint effort—as in, communicate about everything. The selection of team captains would make or break the race. The TWS was strenuous enough without depending on a complete stranger.

This woman didn't seem the outdoorsy type at all. How would she anticipate their needs, much less boost their morale? The looks she and Silas exchanged explained the morale part. On his end, anyway.

Nat blew a breath upward onto her damp forehead. No doubt Twinkle Eyes would see to all Silas's needs, leaving Nat to fend for herself.

A growl pushed its way up her throat. Her displeasure itched to make itself known, but she caught it in time. Acting like kids had landed them in this mess. Summoning her sweetest smile, she ignored Silas's wary look.

"Oh, dealing with both of us"—Nat added the teensiest emphasis to *us*—"will be taxing. At any rate, the rules allow more than one TC. I'm sure my brother will be happy to help us." Her lips curved at the way Silas's jaw flexed at the mention of Jesse.

Bill had been petting the dog while watching the three of them with lively interest. He spoke, "I know my way around the TWS, Miss Nat. If you need a team captain, I'll do it. I'll help shuttle with practice runs too."

Nat shot him a grateful smile. "I might just take you up on your kind offer, Bill." For all her bluster, she'd already concluded Jesse wouldn't make the best TC. The man got overprotective in the span of a paddle push. Now at least they had another option—three if she dared count on Lacy's help.

The river would sooner dry up.

CHAPTER FIVE

"Even if you can't commit to being a co-captain, your presence at some checkpoints would help. Two of us in the boat was your big idea." Nat grimaced. A new low, begging her older brother to hang around. She prided herself on being independent. However, this canoe race had riled every insecurity she possessed. No, the insecurity had started before this latest prank-turned-fiasco. Jesse's townhouse had become her refuge after she'd ghosted Colin. Now she sat eating dinner with her brother as if they hadn't lived apart for the last ten years.

Jesse apparently thought her behavior strange too. The grooves lining his forehead deepened. "I'll do my best. You know I'm on twenty-four-hour call with Mr. Spence, Rory, and a list of contractors. If you want the new rehab wing to stay on schedule ..." He chewed a bite of the chicken she'd grilled. Kept chewing. Then washed it down with a large gulp of iced tea.

Getting the rehab building functional couldn't happen fast enough. If she was still in the running. In the meantime, she and Silas simply had to complete "the world's toughest canoe race." The saliva in her mouth dried up. No pressure there.

Her thoughts drifted back to Colin. Leaving him with no explanation had forced her into exile from her apartment. Jesse had insisted she move in with him until she decided what to do next. If only he knew the entire story. Jesse assumed he was providing refuge from a manipulative ex-boyfriend. The truth proved much more complicated. Colin ran a high-end drug racket. When they'd dated, his shifty behavior had been enough to make her curious, so she'd spied on him. She'd been uber-careful, but what if he found out she knew? What if he wanted to shut her up? Those questions kept her awake at night.

Nat glanced about at Jesse's careless masculine décor. She'd hated the idea of hiding, though wisdom dictated not living alone with her ex still on the loose. Since Jesse had already proved himself a deterrent, Colin wouldn't bother her here.

She'd been so naïve. Hopefully, Colin would chalk her up as a loss. She'd certainly moved on. Hopefully, he would too. She gazed at the unappetizing dinner. Jesse's words brought her back to the present.

"What's this really about? You love paddling. How does one more person in the boat change anything?"

She turned aside. Jesse had way too much experience reading her face. Because Silas didn't count as just one more person. He drove her bonkers with his half smirk. His smoky eyes held secrets she longed to discover. Floundering how to answer, she focused on dissecting an undercooked Brussels sprout. A sharp steak knife would be handy.

"It's just ... the whole Colin-thing messed with me. Another guy so soon ... in such tight quarters. I don't know if I can handle it."

Jesse eyed her as if he didn't quite buy her explanation. Finally, he let out a prolonged breath. "Silas isn't the controlling type. I wouldn't have suggested the event if I suspected he would act any other way than decent.

"Big Gun came in here breathing fire. He wanted to let both of you go, so I had to come up with something fast. Be thankful he latched onto the canoe racing idea. He's gone a step further and wants a Peeps' promo planned around it. You have to follow through. There's no other option."

Nat shifted in the chair, trying not to squirm. "I hear you. I'm grateful you went to bat for us. Neither of us was playing with a full deck at the time." What she wouldn't give for a do-over of the awful scene in the deli. She ground her teeth in frustration. Sometimes she showed the maturity of a tadpole.

One side of her mouth lifted at Jesse's vigorous nod. "I get the feeling Lacy wants to be his girlfriend." Considering the vibes Lacy gave off, Nat found it difficult to imagine being friends with the woman, even if Silas wasn't in the picture.

"I get it. It's not easy being the one who doesn't have somebody." Jesse's voice had gentled, assuring her of his empathy.

"It's hard," Nat admitted. She stabbed the air with her finger, anticipating his next words. "However, it's far better to be lonesome than to have the wrong somebody. You've certainly told me that often enough."

One beetle-black brow quirked. "Let the right man come to you, Nat. Forget about all the others. Surrender your natural desire for love and companionship. Watch God bring him right to you. It'll be so obvious you can't miss it."

"You mean like the night Brenna fell in your lap?" Nat couldn't resist the soft goad. No one in their small group would ever forget Jesse and Brenna's epic meet. While serving at a restaurant, Brenna spilled a tray of salads all over him, but it didn't stop there. She topped it off by falling into his lap.

A toothy grin etched across his face. "You betcha." His smile dimmed. "But back to the boat race. Nat, I know you want to run all-things-business in the new rehab wing. I'm behind you, however unorthodox the methods. Hon, don't allow negative emotions to keep you from achieving your dream. Think of the Texas Water Safari as a business deal. You need to make it work with Silas and Lacy, even if they aren't your favorite people."

"Jess, the TWS timeframe is anywhere from forty-something hours upward to ninety. A hundred hours is the cutoff. A lot of time to 'make it work.'"

Jesse's mouth slanted into a scowl at her air-quote. "What's this really about, Nat?"

She couldn't very well tell him how intriguing she found Silas. Or how it gnawed at her to watch Lacy flirt with him. Or that she didn't trust herself not to make a stupid move out of jealousy.

Instead of verbalizing her massive insecurities, Nat stood, placing the utensils on her plate. Much of her chicken remained uneaten. "Who in our group knows how to grill chicken? Besides me?" A giggle broke loose at the blatant lie. Jesse's playful grimace confirmed it.

As she moved toward the kitchen, he squeezed her affectionately around the waist. "You need to have faith the right guy will come, bug."

Nat leaned into him. She adored his sincere, tender side. Jesse had been her hero since before she could walk or talk. During his deployment, he'd sent letters whenever he could. He'd always kept up with her.

"In the meantime, focus, grasshopper. *Row, row, row your boat. Gently down the stream ...*" His tuneless rendition sounded similar to a donkey's bray. She made a face and covered her eyes. For all his good looks, he couldn't sing a lick.

An odd thought stunned her as she sashayed to the sink, hands full of their plates.

What if the right guy came in a boat?

SILAS CALLED OUT, "If we're going to be competitive, we have to paddle as if we're extensions of each other." He rephrased it, since he'd been saying the same thing for over an hour. They'd chosen a fairly straightforward route on the lower Guadalupe River for their first training run together, specifically to work on stroke rate. Now they were paddling under the bridge at Cheapside. They'd gone ten miles so far, with another twenty to go. The showy green foliage on the banks beckoned him to take a break. He persisted. She had to learn this.

"I heard you the first time." Nat's posture had stiffened. A sign of irritation. Usually with him. "I'll adjust. Give me a minute to get up to speed."

"We don't have a minute." He barked back.

"We have plenty of minutes. If you don't quit the harping, I'm going to knock this paddle upside your head." Nat slung an oar of water back at him for good measure.

Silas dodged, getting wet anyway. He expelled a sigh. One month. One short month, and the race would happen, ready or not. They needed speed. The idea they might not measure up fried him worse than the searing sun. He gazed at the cloudless sapphire sky. A perfect day, if not for the blazing heat, though he simply had to get over it. His skin abhorred the sun. But Nat? Her lovely olive-toned skin soaked it up. She turned brown as an acorn while he resembled a sickly pink tomato.

"Where'd you learn how to stroke?" h e hollered.

Her back arched. "YouTube videos. Where'd you learn?"

"Gramps. With a few tweaks on your stroke, you'll go much faster."

She turned back at him, a scowl twisting her face, "It's always about faster with you, isn't it? Don't you ever relax? Why can't you simply enjoy the journey?"

He drove his blade into the water. "TWS is a race, Nat. We're supposed to be competitive."

She shot him another dark look. "Not the way you go about it. I'm different, Silas. If there's no fun, I'll find a way out."

She'd bail if it wasn't fun? Lots of things were no fun. "Life's not a blast all the time."

"It's not about being a stick-in-the-mud either." The words drifted over her shoulder. Her posture stayed perfect, arms ramrod straight as she maneuvered the paddle.

Was that how she interpreted him? Silas fumed, recognizing himself in her words. Only he didn't know how to fix it. Except pray. Fine. By the time they were done with this event—if it happened—he'd be a different kind of warrior. Not one who fought physically. He'd fight on his knees because he desperately needed *not* to be the person Nat saw.

They paddled in silence for miles. He hollered instructions, but she mostly ignored him. Once, she tossed him a granola bar, the sum total of their communication. So he used the time to pray.

Hours passed. They finally paddled to their pre-arranged destination at the Cuero checkpoint. Not his favorite because of the stink. The landscape repeated what they'd observed the last few hours. Steep banks and the river channel ran through the scads of overhanging trees rife with creepy crawlers.

Nat hopped out of the canoe on shaky legs, stretching her arms. Silas tore his eyes away from her shapely figure and concentrated on bringing the boat in. All right. It wouldn't hurt to extend an olive branch.

At least, that's what kept coming to him as he prayed. Especially since she remained peeved about what she referred to as his micromanaging.

Before she headed to her car, which she'd insisted on bringing, he said, "Dinner? We can debrief … air our grievances?" One side of his mouth tilted upward at her look of shock.

Recovering quickly, she said, "If you're willing to try vegan, I'm all in." Her head angled, as if to weigh his response.

Whatever. He could tolerate plant food if it would restore her … them. "Okay. Just so it's not too weird." He couldn't stomach cauliflower tacos, no matter how noble his intentions.

CHAPTER SIX

Nat suppressed a snicker. Silas's bushy brows knit as he stared at the menu in part confusion, part dismay. Olivia's Café didn't even classify as hard-core vegan.

"I'm afraid to ask for suggestions." He favored her with a wry look.

"The white bean veggie hash is great—lots of protein—the basil Thai rice with tofu is also excellent."

His lips thinned. "No tofu."

"Have you ever tried it? If it's cooked right, it almost tastes like meat."

His frown deepened. "It's cheating to make a plant taste like meat. Meat tastes like meat."

Nat found Silas's philosophy narrow, even if it had a fraction of validity. Much as she enjoyed plant food, it tasted best when it wasn't imitating another food group. "You said you would try vegan food."

"How about a compromise? What if I take a couple of bites of anything you order … and I order chicken fried rice?" Silas's expression had both pleading and virtuous components.

Well ... baby steps. Probably healthier than his usual Big Mac and boatload of fries, all processed within an inch of their greasy lives. "You'll try my food with an open mind?"

"Yes. I also promise to swallow because spitting out nasty vegan food would defeat the purpose." The side of his mouth turned up in a roguish grin.

Nat giggled at his mock-piety. It grew into a belly laugh she found hard to turn off. When the server came for their orders, she could barely control her mirth. Which, of course, meant Silas ordered a non-vegan dish.

Once their food came, he did indeed try some of hers. Satisfied, she knuckled down to business. "Since you called this impromptu dinner a debrief, let's talk shop about the race."

Silas's hazel eyes darkened with an emotion Nat couldn't read. "You don't care for my training methods." It wasn't a question.

She forked a bite of her hash. "Whatever. You need the assurance I agree with the faster stroke rate." She munched, enjoying the blend of kale and legumes. "It's the only way we'll be competitive—I get it. You also know I'm a personal trainer. It's my job to help people accomplish their health goals. That said, there's always an aspect of strength training because strength is a tremendous asset to a person's overall health."

Momentarily distracted by the blond scruff along his jaw, she dove deep to find her concentration again. "I'm committed to a faster stroke rate. Because of my feminine physique, however, I'll never have your level of strength. It's the way God made me. If you'll be patient, though, I'll improve. And I believe we'll reach the sweet spot we need for competition."

"In the meantime, I need to back off with telling you how to paddle." Silas's countenance drooped.

"We won't get faster in one day or overnight. I'll keep track of our times, because" She pummeled her fists on the table, imitating a drumroll. "in about four weeks, you'll love our new stroke rate."

Silas smiled in spite of his concerns. "Here's hoping. Pretty obvious the fear of failure follows me around, huh?" He'd polished off his food five minutes ago. Now he held his fork in the air and pointed to her half-eaten plate. She gave him a questioning look.

The grin appeared again, along with a sheepish expression. "I'm still hungry, and your white veggie stuff isn't half bad."

Laughing, she slid her plate over to him. He wolfed it down as if he were starving. Once he'd swallowed the last bite, he pushed the plate away.

"What you said makes all kinds of sense. Sorry about my overbearing attitude—side effect of being in charge." His gaze made her shiver. "You don't need to apologize for your 'feminine physique' ever again. I'll take you in the boat over a beefy meathead any day."

She arched a brow. "If that was supposed to be a compliment, you've got a long way to go, Sy." A measure of satisfaction filled her as he ducked his head with ... What? Embarrassment? Served him right. She cleared her throat. Might as well get it over with. "There's another thing ... we need to decide on the team captains." She steeled for an argument.

Silas gazed at her thoughtfully. "Yeah, we do. You heard Gramps volunteer. He'd hate me saying this, but I'm not sure he's up to it."

"What happened to Lacy?"

"She only wants to tag along. Said being a team captain would suck the fun out of it."

No surprise there. Nat worked to keep her facial features under control. Gloating wouldn't help. "Okay. Gramps is a good choice with backup." Might as well get it over with. "Jesse won't commit either."

Silas drew out a breath, obviously relieved. "Okay. Two negatives, one willing. We still need another person."

"I've been mulling over it. You'd think we'd know plenty of people, considering we work at Peeps, but I keep drawing a blank."

"Me too." An idea occurred to him. "Hey, what if I check with Pastor Mike? He's peppered me with questions about our practice runs. He followed the race last year. Even used an illustration in one of his sermons."

"Yeah, I remember. An analogy about the race being akin to our journey with Christ. His plate stays so full he has to plan downtime into his schedule. It'd be worth asking, though. If he can't, he might know of someone else. He has oodles of contacts."

Before they left the restaurant, Silas hedged. Finally, he said, "About getting faster …" He held up his hands. "This is only a suggestion. I'm not trying to micromanage." He eyed her as if she were an unpredictable toddler. "I've got videos I watch to review my paddling skills. You're welcome to watch them with me. Gramps is always available. He adores yakking about paddle technique."

Well, for the love … She mustered a concerned look, then placed a hand on his forehead. She enjoyed the way his skin wrinkled under her hand.

"What?" he asked.

"Just wondering if you're sick." A smile teased at the corners of her mouth. "What a sweet suggestion. It sounded almost contrite. Are you all right?"

"I'm fine." It came out growly, yet the corner of his lip tugged upward.

"Well, good." She said airily, around the hitch in her throat. "Wouldn't want you lagging too far behind."

CHAPTER SEVEN

troke. Stroke. Stroke. Silas cast another look at the darkening sky. This stretch of river between the Swinging Bridge and Tivoli stayed unpredictable. With the low water levels, their practice run through the logjam cut had become crucial.

Their subsequent training runs had surprisingly gone well. Nat's predictions had proved true. He'd gotten more realistic about their progression. She'd worked hard to lengthen her strokes. Their boat balance had improved with each run. At the beginning, he'd hoped she'd quit. Now he almost looked forward to their canoe time. Almost. Ignoring his attraction to her helped.

Trees on the banks swished as the wind picked up. The air held the scent of rain. Nat's floppy hat had blown off her head moments ago. A few escapees from her ponytail danced in the gusts. A crack of lightning landed somewhere close. She flinched and kept paddling. Rain pinged on the water, big drops at first, then more.

Drat. They'd made good time up to this point. The wet

weather would slow things down. Cold white marbles pelted the boat and stung his skin.

"Nat," he yelled to be heard over the gusts. At his motion, she steered toward the bank. Another lightning strike lit up the sky. Too close. The hail, now golf ball-sized, still struck with sharp enough force they should seek cover. But where? Nothing but trees around, and they weren't an option.

"What do we do?" Nat shouted. Rain plastered her hair down and streamed off her high cheekbones. Still breathtakingly pretty.

Back to the question for which Silas had no solution. No picnic table to hide under ... no deserted outbuilding ... Gramps waited for them miles down the river.

Nat pointed downward. "The boat! We use the boat." She jumped out of the canoe. In a flash, Silas grabbed his end. Together, they inverted the narrow canoe, holding it over their heads.

"On three, we go down." Nat nodded as he counted. Gingerly, they lowered the boat over themselves on the muddy bank. They crouched, then scrabbled onto their knees. Facing each other, they wrestled the sides of the boat down.

The noise of the hail hitting the carbon-fiber hull was deafening. Nat's eyes scrunched closed, jaws flexed. Silas gritted his teeth just in case they decided to fly out of his mouth. How did they go from barely able to stand each other to huddling under a boat? The heat from her wet body stirred a long-buried desire. Slowly, the noise receded. His arms ached from gripping the boat.

"You good?" he asked.

She nodded, awarding him a weak smile. "Yes. Not sure how I'll get up, though." Her arms wobbled. The boat slid lower, almost covering her face.

"We got this." Silas inserted a note of confidence he

didn't feel. "First, one leg." He clumsily swung a muddy leg forward, planting it on the ground, then nodded to her. She followed. He repeated the movement, then stayed in a crouch to give her time to make a similar move. Slowly, they rose, still holding the boat. The rain had dwindled to sparse drips. The hail ceased the imitation of loose pinballs. Without planning it, they moved in sync, setting the upside-down boat on the ground. He quickly checked for holes, pleased to find only minor dings in the hull. Didn't account for the shadow he'd perceived since they emerged from under the boat.

He glanced around the area, trying to find the source of the uneasiness gripping him. The atmosphere seemed too still. Wind and lightning had broken off tree limbs. Tree trunks had cracked into odd shapes. Even the *whoo whoo* from a river owl sounded ominous.

Nat rubbed her arms. Silas's prickly skin morphed into a shiver.

Well, of course. His sense of something off ranked as nothing more than cold skin because of the temperature drop. He moved closer to Nat, putting an arm around her shoulder. At her surprised look, he gave her a squeeze. "If we're going to make it down the river, we'll have to share body heat."

Despite the encouraging words, his sniper training kept alerting. Someone had been watching them.

THE CLOSENESS SILAS instigated had been about getting down the river, not anything else. *Think about it, girl.* Their physical condition, soaking wet and muddy as the bank they sat on, didn't quite make for a romantic interlude.

As her thoughts veered toward practicality, Silas brushed

something from her forehead, lips parted in his adorable half smirk. "You're wearing mud."

Apart from jostling his shoulder, she looked away. Just to let him know he couldn't get to her. An awkward silence ensued, except he didn't remove his arm. Since they were this close ... she might not get another opportunity. Silas slid away from a serious topic faster than the hailstorm they'd just experienced.

"Sy, I know we've got to get down the river today, but I keep getting the feeling you're going to bail on the race. Am I wrong?"

Silas kept staring at the trees. Belatedly, it seemed, he turned his attention to what she said. "Bailing? I've thought about it."

"How will we keep our jobs, our futures, if we don't do the race?" Fear clawed at her insides, but she strived for a reasonable tone.

"Yeah," he conceded. "I can't get around it either." He faced her, seeming to choose his words carefully. "Best I can figure out, I'm mad about not getting a choice in the matter. I'm still working through why. Lord knows the military doesn't do choices. The Ten Commandments aren't suggestions either. They're rules."

A giggle bubbled up in her throat. "So you've been listening in church." Her words turned somber. "Except we broke the rules when we acted like two-year-olds. That's why we didn't get a choice."

His forehead creased into ruts. "I know. If I were in Jesse and Mr. Spence's shoes, I'd have outright fired us. As it is, I'm still wrestling with not having a choice. Grateful hasn't happened yet."

She inclined her head a notch. "So the vibe I'm getting is you trying *not* to bail?"

Resignation streaked across his features. "Probably."

She looked away, then blew out a sigh. "I struggle too. On gloomy days"—she waved at their damp, dripping surroundings—"I wish we didn't have to do it either."

A low chuckle rose in his chest. His fathomless hazel eyes held hers. "How do you keep going?"

She scrambled up, missing the warmth of his shoulder. Her hands landed on her hips. "I pop any negative attitude in the nose. If I want my future at Peeps, it's simple. I choose to move forward. I do it as many times as I have to. What keeps you going?"

"You." His look of astonishment clearly communicated it was the last thing in the universe he'd planned to say.

She couldn't bear it if he bungled an apology too. "Wrong answer, Tonto. You want your future at Peeps as much as I want mine. It's the only reason we're in a boat together for four days, right?"

"Right." His immediate echo combined with the relief coursing through his expression convinced her he'd misspoken. She took a deep breath. For a second, he'd almost fooled her into thinking he cared.

Guard your heart, sister. She ruthlessly stuffed away her increasingly tender feelings toward him. They'd made a business deal. She needed to treat it as such. Even if it left her feeling flat, and more than a little rejected.

CHAPTER EIGHT

"Nat, you have to consume more than avocadoes. You'll get weak, then what will happen?" Silas shifted on the pew, shooting a prayer to heaven. It had been his bright idea they go over checklists after the Wednesday night service. After their slight bit of transparency on the river, he'd assumed she'd be more reasonable. He should have known nothing had changed. Prettier than any other woman he'd ever seen, she also appeared the most stubborn. And now bristling like a porcupine. Yep. Brilliant idea.

"Plant food and a steady supply of protein shakes will get me through. Strenuous activity zaps my appetite. What are you going to do?" She leaned toward him to peer at the list he held. "There isn't much on your list in the way of food or supplements."

Silas had previously caught tantalizing whiffs of her fresh citrus fragrance. It swelled to the point he could hardly think. "I'll get whatever I need. If you're willing to share your energy supps, that works for me."

The questioning arc of her brow disappeared as she jotted a note on her list. "Got it. Plenty of Spiz and Gu."

His eyes narrowed. "I'm afraid to ask what those are."

"Spiz is a meal-replacement. It's basically a protein shake. Gu packets are energy gel shots to squirt in your mouth. Lots of different flavors. Minimum fuss, maximum benefit." Her pecan-colored eyes sparkled with mischief.

"They sound disgusting."

"They're not so bad once you've done it a few times."

Still sounded awful. He gazed at his list again. Anywhere to keep his mind off her pink lips. "I prefer real food," he finally said.

"Me too," she admitted. "Except for I don't know how long I'll maintain the energy to paddle *and* digest real food—much less the kind you eat."

There she went again, harping on his fondness for fast food. Any softening on his part vanished. "Glitter Girl, if we're going to do this thing, you need to quit lecturing me on the horrors of poor nutrition."

They stared at each other. Silas sighed, exasperated with this beautiful woman who wouldn't back down a gnat's whisker. Nat had been aptly named—her ability to pester a soul proved endless. He hadn't the foggiest notion of what he'd been thinking with his "you keep me going" answer. Going cuckoo. At least she'd acted as if it were no big deal. Nat had become a complication his solitary life simply couldn't afford.

"So, you guys ready for the big canoe race this weekend?" They both started guiltily, then exchanged a look.

When neither answered, Pastor Mike said cheerfully, "Hm. Looks as if we need to pray."

"What we need is a team captain," Nat blurted.

Pastor Mike's dark eyes lit as he slid sideways into the pew in front of them. He extended his hands to Silas and Nat. "I'm interested. Let's pray first."

Silas took Nat's hand, trying not to think about how soft it felt. As Pastor Mike prayed, Silas's aggravation slowly faded. The man had a knack for communicating. His words flowed effortlessly. Peace filled Silas as his warped perspective realigned with God. No matter how it came about, the Texas Water Safari represented an opportunity to grow in character. Still, he couldn't resist mentally tacking on a small prayer of his own. *Give me plenty of patience, Lord. Because I'm sure going to need it sharing a canoe with Nat.*

IN A SOFT MURMUR, Nat repeated Pastor Mike's amen. It eased her soul to remember she didn't have to do this all by herself. God would help them. Shortly after she'd cut off things with Colin, she'd renewed her commitment to live for Christ in this very place. Silas made a similar commitment the same month. Nat hoped he'd be open to talking about it. She could certainly use some pointers. Somewhere along the line, she'd acquired a talent for mucking things up. Silas held himself together way better than she did. Fifty-plus hours of paddling rivers—hopefully, some deep conversations would happen along the way.

"Are you serious about the job as Team Captain?" Silas directed the question to Pastor Mike.

The tall man nodded with a wry look. "I adore competitive sports, as you well know from my sermons. That said, I've always found 'the world's toughest canoe race' intriguing. Let me run it by my wife. She helps keep my sports obsession in check. I'm guessing there's more to it than pats on the back and handing out water jugs."

Silas and Nat exchanged an are-you-thinking-what-I'm-thinking look, then Nat said, "Yeah, definitely more. We'll need to go over things."

The silver streaks in Pastor Mike's black hair shimmered as he rose from the pew. He paused in the aisle. "I'll get back to you once I've talked to Lindsey. We'll get together soon, depending on her yay or nay." He favored them with a brilliant smile. "It's a grueling race from what I understand. I'll be praying for you no matter what." A deacon headed his way. "Duty calls. More later." He cut through a pew to intercept the man.

The deep groove in Silas's forehead had faded to a faint horizontal line. "He wants to do it. Does God answer prayer that fast?"

Nat hopped up from the padded bench, still reeling on the inside. "It's as if He knew what we needed before we prayed." She'd puzzle over it later. "Walk with me to the foyer? I got you something for the Safari."

Silas's sandy brows knit together. "For me?"

His look of disbelief sliced into her self-esteem. Was she really so awful he couldn't imagine her doing something nice? She attempted to brush it off. Forging ahead had become the only way she knew how to make things happen. "C'mon, silly. You'll see."

Her boots click-clacked on the foyer's hardwood floor, echoing her nervousness. She reached for a duffle bag she'd stashed in the corner. Lifting out a straw cowboy hat, she plunked it on her head. Then she pulled out another one and extended it to Silas. "It's yours if you want it. The wide brim will provide more sun protection." The look of amazement on his face had her backing up in full retreat. "If you don't care for it—"

"No!" He hastily stepped forward, taking the hat. "It's a great idea."

Silas shook back the shaggy hair hanging over one eye. He adjusted the hat around his ears. "I've always wanted one of these." He took it off and examined the inside. "The thin lining gives it serious UV protection. The leather strap will keep the wind from blowing it away." A rare smile creased his craggy face. "This is perfect, Nat. Glad you thought of it."

His words of praise caused her stomach to unclench. She put a hand on her chin, pretending to scrutinize his appearance. "Have to admit, it looks pretty good on you, cowboy." She deliberately batted her eyelashes. Belatedly, she hoped he'd realize she wasn't serious. An inward groan threatened to make itself heard. Her days of flirty come-ons ended once she'd started back to church. Flirting had been fun. She'd enjoyed the powerful feelings that accompanied it … until she snared Colin. At first, he'd been quite the trophy … then the isolation and the smothering started.

Silas's low chuckle made her pulse increase. "The, um, *hat* looks good on you too."

Warmth stole around her neck. His phrasing verged on flirty. Surely, she imagined it. He'd been cornered into putting up with her so they could both move forward with their jobs.

The silly flutter in her heart persisted.

CHAPTER NINE

The banana-colored moon proved irresistible. So much so, Nat chose it over duty. She scootered along the open road, cherishing the quiet night. Away from the noisy bustle of TWS registration. Away from Jesse's worried gaze, the questions in Silas's eyes, and Lacy's tinkling prattle. Gramps' steadfastness had gotten her through dinner. Then she'd begged off from anymore togetherness.

A cool breeze had ushered in the evening. Giving in to its siren call, Nat skipped the meeting with Silas and Pastor Mike for one last pow-wow about the race. Silas would handle it. She'd trade his ongoing disapproval for this enchanting night. The wind stinging her face scattered the brain clutter she'd endured this past week. She needed this, no matter if the uneven rumble of her scooter overtook the cicada song she'd hoped to hear.

The hills of central Texas rolled gently. A sweet variation from the flat plains of Valiant. The road ahead ribboned into the twinkly horizon. Stars glittered brightly, away from the city lights. A few vehicles had passed. Mostly she'd been alone, reveling in the thrum of her motor scooter.

Until distant headlights closed in. Fear slammed into her gut when the glare in her side mirrors blinded her. The greasy smell of fuel turned her stomach sour. The vehicle rumbled louder. Faster. She gripped the handles, accelerating. Then a deer darted out of nowhere, straight into her path.

Nat swerved to a side road, skidding on a patch of loose gravel. Losing control, she fell to the left. The bike collapsed on her right side. Dazed, she saw the truck slow. A face peered out from the passenger window. A mean grin poked through a beard and mustache.

Mouth dry, she swallowed. Terror held her voice captive. She didn't move until the face disappeared. A tiny corner of her mind tucked away details. A dark monster truck. The kind a person had to climb up into. Menacing. License plate, BHR—. Foreboding washed through her. With trembly arms, she pushed the scooter away. Pain tore through her body as she rose. Nausea swam through her. She dropped to her knees, promptly emptying the contents of her stomach into the dusty swirl of gravel.

She slowly examined herself for injuries. A nasty road rash on one arm. Her back and side ached abominably. Head, legs, and feet were still in working order for the moment. Sore wouldn't begin to describe how she'd feel tomorrow.

Oh, no. The race. The idea of paddling a canoe made her want to hurl again. *Help.* She needed help. Patting a pocket for her phone, she pulled it out. No signal. Just as well. Jesse would jump into big-brother mode faster than she slid off the road.

A deer popping out of nowhere happened frequently. The truck crowding her? Not so much. It was incredibly careless or …

Not wanting to finish the thought, Nat picked up the

scooter. No use assigning sinister motives, since she had no evidence. Better to focus on the canoe race. If she wanted to secure her future, the pain would have to stay well hidden.

She'd pray all the way back. God would hear. All would be well. A shiver wrapped around her spine despite the warm night.

SILAS KNEELED NEXT to the boat, securing the bilge pump with Gorilla tape. Once he finished, he hunkered down in the grassy shade of the huge live oaks. In every available space, people loaded canoes with supplies for the race. Lacy sat on a nearby picnic table bench, looking at her phone. He'd suffered through worse company. They'd laughed and had a good visit driving in from Valiant. Still, his hope for a chat with Nat on the eve of the race hadn't materialized. She'd made herself scarce all evening, saying she preferred solitude. Since when? Nat was an extrovert clear to the bone.

Where was she, anyway? He tugged at the strap of the cowboy hat she'd given him. He'd put it on shortly after dressing so he wouldn't forget it.

"Hey."

He swiveled. "Hey, yourself." His breath came out in a rush. The woman who'd taken over his thoughts shaped up as gorgeous, even while dressed in unflattering attire. The white sport leggings many participants wore to guard against the heat and water weren't pretty on anyone. Respect for her rose a notch. She'd come to compete, not make a fashion statement.

She gazed at him for a long minute, then she walked around to the other side of the boat and lowered herself onto the grass. Slowly. Most unlike Nat.

Something Silas couldn't identify shafted into his soul.

"What can I do?" she asked. She looked at the canoe. "Who did this?" She pointed to the team name alongside of the boat. "Glitter and the Grouch?"

"Gramps's idea. He painted it on the sly."

Nat smiled wanly. "Guess he figured us out, huh?"

Lacy had strolled over, phone in hand. "Hi, Nat. Silas, are you okay with me taking pictures?"

"Uh, sure. Do you have the clipboard with the checklist?"

"Yes." Lacy's look lingered on the cowboy hat trailing down Nat's back, identical to his. Then she made for the picnic table.

The air buzzed with occasional shouts and lively conversations. Officials made pathways through the canoes with clipboards, shaking hands with race participants. The stifling heat made Silas look forward to the river water. His lips scrunched sideways. Soon enough, he'd be wishing for dry land.

Jesse strode in their direction with his usual frown. Did the guy ever relax? Silas stood, dusting the grass from his swim trunks, and stepped over to meet him as Lacy handed the clipboard to Nat. He'd loaded the supplies. Nat was supposed to check them against the list.

She'd handle it. Nat managed whatever she set her mind to. If she didn't lose focus.

Jesse observed him with a penetrating gaze. Time to make nice. Silas stuck out his hand.

"You got this?" Jesse asked.

Silas nodded. Jesse had said little to him since the incident in the deli. But then, his boss had never been the chatty type, and Silas refused to suck up.

"I need your word that you'll look out for Nat. She's young ... and isn't her usual perky self." Jesse's eyes bored into him, then he expelled a sharp breath. "I don't know what's going on."

So her brother had noticed too. The uneasiness Silas detected earlier burrowed deeper. He shrugged. "No one ever knows how they'll hold up after three days of non-stop paddling. Marathon canoes races are mentally and physically challenging. It's probably nerves. You know her better than I do." Silas paused as Jesse's jaw tightened, conveying frustration with her as well. The insight settled some of Silas's personal angst about Nat. "I'll take care of her. No worries."

"If she lets you do that, you'll be the first." Jesse said dryly. "Knowing you've got her back helps." He turned on his heel and strode back the way he came. Tall, rangy build. A natural leader. All the things Silas would never be.

The rumors he'd heard about how much the man loved his sister hadn't been exaggerated. Silas got the distinct impression he might lose a body part if anything happened to her. They were partners, but Jesse's entreaty—even if it came across as a command—sounded as if he meant more than the upcoming race.

Message received, Boss.

THE HEAT BLAZED hotter than the proverbial oven. The three pain relief tablets Nat had taken were making a dent. She slowly raised her left arm above her head and stretched.

Bet that hurts like a son of a gun.

Strange those words should pop into her mind. Most of her memories of Dad didn't bring warm, fuzzy feelings. Still, she remembered him saying those exact words. He'd often commiserated with her childhood bumps and bruises. Despite the pain—she ached from head to toe—she treasured the memory. The forgiveness she'd been practicing toward her father was bearing fruit. Pastor Mike had promised it would happen. Dad wouldn't know, having died several years ago, but a gentle sweetness replaced the bitter feelings she'd held on to for years. Progress. She tucked it away for later. A far more pleasant thing to dwell on than how much she hurt. She tramped over to Silas, who frowned at a chart of the racing pathway.

"Are you ready to tackle the river? We're sticking to the plan, right?" Nat asked. Silas pierced her with a look as if probing for weak spots. She lifted her chin in silent challenge. Would she ever be enough for this man? Finally, he nodded.

Their strategy struck her as deceptively simple. For this first quarter, Silas proposed they find their stride quickly, then stick to it, come what may. Nat agreed in theory, then prayed for the ability to stay with the blistering pace he was sure to set. Making their way back to the boat, they stopped to talk to acquaintances. It had created a buzz once their intention to race together became known. Changing from solo to tandem was an unusual move. Whenever someone asked why, they stayed mum. The fallout from their prank-gone-wrong deserved no explanation.

"Ready to roll?" Nat took hold of the line attached to the bow. Silas shook his head and walked toward her.

"Wanna pray?" For the first time, Nat spotted a glimmer of something other than secrets in Silas's deep hazel eyes. He held out a hand as if daring her to refuse.

She stepped closer to take it. His much larger hand enveloped hers, surprising her with how right it felt. The lively buzz of excited participants faded. "You go first?"

A smile lit his face as they bowed their heads. "Lord, I'm new at praying, yet I get the distinct impression we're going to need Your help before it's all done. Thanks for Nat's willingness to do this with me. Please keep us safe on the river ... and always."

When he paused, Nat picked up the thread. "I'm thankful for Silas, despite him winning the toss for the first stern stint." She nudged him. "He's right, God. We're countin' on Your help to get us to the finish line." She gently squeezed his hand, then released it and stepped away.

Silas's maddening half-smirk appeared. The man actually looked happy. Here they were, about to start the biggest ordeal of their lives. And he'd asked her to pray with him. Her heart swelled with contentment. Spilling over with enthusiasm, she raised a palm. "We can do this!"

He slapped back a hearty high five, then stepped to the stern. "I got this."

Hands on hips, she said, "Not all the time, you don't."

Silas didn't miss a beat. "I know, Glitter Girl. I know."

CHAPTER TEN

Voices counted down: *Three, two, one*, then the starting horn blared at Spring Lake in San Marcos. Their narrow canoe rubbed against the cement embankment. Silas gritted his teeth. Not where he wanted to start. Because they hadn't run the prelim together, their placement tumbled to dead last. Silas sliced powerful strokes through the water. In the bow, Nat followed his lead, paddling furiously through the chaotic jumble of canoes, trying to navigate their way around the slower boats.

Thrashing his paddle, Silas worked each watery crevice to their advantage with an aggression bordering on brutal. He nosed between a sharp corner and another boat, pleased that Nat anticipated his moves. Water splashed on all sides, sprinkling them with drops. The sun pummeled them with heat. Exhilarated by the hot watery ride, he worked hard to fall in behind a multi-man team moving as if made of quicksilver, opening up a clear path toward the first island portage. He steered around a rock, shooting a glance behind him. They'd passed a multitude of boats. Nat still wore her cowboy hat, while his trailed down his back, bedraggled rat-style. Nat looked athletic and feminine in hers.

BAM! Another canoe slammed into his daydreams, right into the stern of their boat. It rocked wildly, then turned sideways. He flung his paddle down, grappling with the sides, trying to steady it. The mix of current and tippy canoe shoved them toward the bank. Water flowed into the boat because the bilge pump couldn't keep up.

The boat capsized before he could react. Warm water enveloped him. Nat screamed. He thrashed around in the water, grabbing hold of the boat. Flinging his head from side to side, he peered around for Nat. Gasping for air, she emerged, latching an arm onto the other end.

"Now what?" she yelled.

"We swim the boat in. I'll lead." He called, pointing to the nearest shoreline.

She nodded. Together they wrestled the heavy, half-submerged boat, swimming in the deep water, staying out of the path of other boats. Finally, Silas touched bottom. Nat helping, they wedged it between rocks on the shore, then turned it sideways. The lively buzz of onlookers made Silas want to hide.

Nat flopped on the ground, panting. She held an arm in the air, victor-style. "And we're off to a great start."

Silas gave her a narrow look. "You think this is funny?"

"You don't?" Humor laced the words. "This race comes with a warning label, *World's Toughest Canoe Race*—what could go wrong?"

Despite his ire, he caught her gist. "I only wish it hadn't started so early."

Nat rose with a grimace, shook out her wet cowboy hat, and placed it back on her head. "Yeah, well, we don't always get what we want, cowboy." She toed the boat. "You think it's still race-worthy?"

Silas ran a hand over the dent just left of the stern, then looked over the boat with a critical eye. "Yes, despite the impact of a stern hook." His gaze snagged on a limp pink blob on the bow and frowned. Nat's girl power flag. When had that happened? He let it pass. For now. "Let's just hope there are no more boat issues."

The glint in her eye promised no such wish. About boat issues. Or girl power.

* * *

THE BOATS HAD THINNED on the glassy river. Yellowish algae crowded the banks in some spots. Brown rocks and gravel stayed visible on the river bottom. The crowds lining the banks to cheer on the boaters had also thinned. Immense trees in full green foliage created the impression of deep, dark forest on both sides of the river. A grin stretched Nat's lips. At last, they were competing.

"Doing all right back there?" Silas shouted above the river rush.

"Yes. Having fun," she called back. Their positions left little room for conversation with all the noise, except they'd promised to work at it. Another strategy tip they'd received— have fun. A race veteran said it would make all the difference.

Nat hoped Silas would get on board with the fun part.

They paddled, frantically making up for lost time. Finally, they reached the island at the end of Spring Lake. Uh-oh. The route they'd planned burgeoned with a jam-packed crowd. Silas had to have seen it. Before the canoe edged to the strip of sand, Nat jumped out of the canoe at the exact time Silas did, only he landed on the bank, while she treaded in chest-deep water. She swam forward, ignoring the ache along her left side.

He pointed. "We go straight up the middle."

Nat finally reached the bank and picked up her end of the canoe. People ahead of them trekked toward the left. "Why not that way?" she asked, motioning toward a path on the far right with less traffic.

"Rocks all over the place. Don't want to risk it." He tugged at the boat.

Low brush scratched at her legs as they hustled through the tall weeds. "Ow." Nat swallowed a moan as she stumbled across another jagged rock. A demanding workout no longer held top billing in the torture department. Doggedly, she hung on to her end, determined to uphold her part—the boat and the bargain they'd made. For the thousandth time, she'd wished the glitter prank had not happened. Though Silas's outrage had almost made it worth it. Almost.

On the other side, the golden-brown water beckoned them, a relief after the hot, sweaty portage. Nat stopped to yank at twigs clinging to her leggings. Silas sat in the boat with a frown. *Keep up. Keep up.* The mantra driving at her, she leaned on a rock to lower into the boat, then grabbed her paddle.

"Rio Vista Dam next," Silas called.

"Got it." She sang back, acting as if they were out on a fun little outing.

If only.

Their paddles chopped through the water as they hurried to pass other canoes. Starting in last place served as disadvantage enough. The stern hook had set them back further.

Nat heard the enthusiastic fan noise before she saw anyone. If possible, Silas had hunkered down lower, intent on ripping through the water as fast as possible. As they navigated a sharp turn, spectators lining both banks cheered.

They had paddled this stretch once in a practice run. The rapids flowed over three separate drops. Nat hopped out of the boat quickly to portage across the first drop. "Let's paddle over the next two," she hollered to Silas.

Shaking his head from side to side, he yelled back, "No way. We'll carry it. Less wear and tear on the boat."

Chicken.

She bellowed a loud, ongoing cluck, much to the amusement of the onlookers.

Silas's look would have withered her skin if the heat didn't beat him to it. "No! We have to save time. If the canoe takes on water, or worse, it'll slow us down."

She stuck out her tongue at his sturdy back, but there remained little else to do except follow his lead. No matter how much her side ached. They jumped out, portaging over the next two rapids. On the last rapid, Nat observed one spectacular wipeout. A canoe in their category wrapped around a submerged rock, breaking into neat halves, ending the race for the participants. Seeing their glum looks, she stiffened her hold on the boat. Grudgingly, she admitted Silas had called it.

After the first bend in the river, the miles blended together. The rest of the morning and early afternoon turned into a blur of steering the sharp turns of the upper San Marcos River while not slowing down and endless portages. By Silas's calculations, they'd carried the canoe across Thompson's Island Dam and Road Bridge, then Cummings Dam. She hardly remembered any of it. Just keeping one foot in front of the other while holding her end of the boat had zapped her energy level.

The low river levels were taking a physical toll. They

worked to find the deeper channels to help them go faster. The river had turned into a creek with very little flow, causing them to paddle over shallow gravel bars. Aside from the "official dam portages," they constantly jumped out of the boat to drag it through shallow spots.

"Cottonseed Rapids ahead at the ten-mile marker," Silas shouted. "How do you want to play it? Portage or paddle?" After Rio Vista, Nat knew the safer route would be to carry the boat around—except she didn't know if her bruised side could take another portage.

"I'm sick of portages. Let's go through!" She'd shouted back over the intensity of the rushing water. Their canoe picked up speed, affording them precious little time to make a different decision. Silas appeared to shrug, then held his oar in two hands over his head. Oh, whoa. A watery rollercoaster ride. Nat sucked in a damp breath. She held her oar high, imitating Silas. At least they'd be in sync in one way.

The boat gradually slid, then shimmied, drenching them with water. Their supplies, though secure, popped up like so many corks. Any control they might have had vanished in the span of a mosquito bite. Leaning left, Silas dropped his hands and struggled to keep the tippy boat upright.

CHAPTER ELEVEN

Thrashing water threatened to separate him from the oar, his only means of support. Desperate, he dug in. "Stay with me," he yelled to Nat. Soon enough, the rapids gave way to rushing water, and they adapted their paddling to stay the course. They'd passed the danger of capsizing again unless something stupid happened, the possibilities of which ranked high.

Nat, struggling for breath and clutching her side, riveted his attention.

"You okay?"

"Yeah." Weariness underscored the word.

"You gonna tell me why your side hurts?"

"Nope." Nat shot him a testy look. "Won't make any difference."

As much as he desired an answer, he only said, "A few more miles to Staples Dam. You hungry?"

Nat shook her head vigorously. Drops of water spewed into the air and fell.

Silas permitted himself a longer-than-usual look at her.

"You workin' up an appetite?" Concern flickered through him at her shrug. She needed to keep her strength up.

They had to keep going. Their futures depended on it.

Once her breathing evened out, they settled into a routine. To his astonishment, Silas found he enjoyed paddling with Nat. As they hurried along, he discovered her presence soothed him. Their oars slid through the water in easy sync. Doing it together added an element he couldn't quite put his finger on.

A memory of his ex-wife surfaced. Early in their marriage, they'd been full of hope. Before the not-so-polite indifference began. Before the sniper missions drained his soul. He shook off the chill pervading his body.

"Staples Dam ahead," Silas pointed. "We'll portage across. Gramps will be on the other side."

Mike would be there too. The pastor's perspective helped Silas find his way forward when past mistakes threatened to pull him under.

Soon enough, they were dragging the boat out of the water. Staples Dam had been cobbled of concrete, stone, and blocks. Plenty of onlookers milled around. Silas didn't miss the worried set of Nat's jaw as she observed the steep ramp.

"Let me go first. Then you'll be at the top to guide the boat." He'd handle the bulk of the boat's weight as it came down.

"I'll let it down easy." Nat gripped the rope in one hand, her end of the canoe in the other. She used her body to help steady it. He started down slowly, holding the rope, taking care to balance the boat over the steep ramp, then down.

She attempted to lower the bulky boat to him in small increments. It slid downhill much faster. Silas hustled backward to control the rest of its journey.

The boat slopped inelegantly into the shallow basin. Once

he had a firm hold, Silas reached into the river for cool water to splash his face and neck. Nat adjusted her sunglasses.

"I see Gramps." Silas trudged to the right bank, rope in hand, pulling the canoe. Nat helped glide the other end along.

Still standing in the water, Gramps waded out to meet him. Elvis followed. "How's it going, Sy?"

Mike handed each of them a baggie, but addressed Nat. "PB and honey—your favorite."

She took the bag, more interested in the bottle of Gatorade. Silas prayed under his breath she'd eat.

Silas gobbled huge bites of his sandwich as he talked to Gramps and petted Elvis. Lacy stood on the bank, taking a picture.

Nat had walked away with a knuckle under her nose after a glimpse of Silas's bologna sandwich. He guessed she didn't care for the pink, processed meat. He'd heard her opinion on the subject often enough. The warm air intensified the smell. Mike had engaged her in conversation. Probably encouraging her to eat. Whatever he said appeared to work because she took a bite, washing it down with Gatorade. Then another. Silas sauntered over as she fed a bite to Elvis.

"The rule is each bite you feed the dog means two for you."

Nat carefully swallowed the bite she'd been chewing. "Doesn't apply because I'm done. Is there a protein drink around?"

Pastor Mike hurried over, shaking a container. "Here you go. Long afternoon ahead."

Silas turned to head back to the boat. He held a hand up as she walked past. She popped him a high five, then climbed into the canoe.

They could do this.

Together.

STROKE. Stroke. Stroke. High overhead, the sun beamed, torching her back. Nat couldn't decide if her body resembled a crispy critter or a soggy noodle. They still moved down the river at a grueling pace, using single-blade paddles. She looked forward to the stretches where double-blades were more efficient. Less navigating around obstacles would ease the constant throbbing on her side.

If only she hadn't gone on a motor scooter ride last night. The desire to get away from the Silas-Lacy twosome and Jesse's overprotectiveness had pushed her into it. Only Jesse hadn't been concerned once Brenna called. When Nat made loud kissing noises, he'd called her a brat, then ordered her out of his room. Despite her achy burning body, the memory afforded a giggle. Big Brother had a multitude of buttons to press. To her everlasting delight, she knew them all.

She and Silas hadn't paddled this stretch of river much because it didn't change. Boring was a better word. "You wanna sing?" She glanced back at Silas, who grunted and kept paddling.

Grouch. The man could use a little livening up. She took a deep breath, belting out the first song that came to mind. "Amazing grace, how sweet the sound, that saved a wretch like meeeee."

She sucked in another breath, picking up where she left off. "I once was lost, but now I'm found ..."

Silas finished the lyrical phrase, though he didn't sing the words. Maybe he wasn't a total dried stick after all.

Stroking faster, they caught up to a canoe with a threesome who'd been leading the last mile or so. "How's it goin'?" Nat asked. No one answered. Nat got the distinct impression they'd been arguing. Personally, she would have enjoyed some conversation. Their stony faces showed it wouldn't happen, so she pushed harder.

Reading Silas. Those dark hazel eyes held secrets. If she existed as the last person on earth, he'd probably still clam up. Frankly, she found his lack of communication maddening. Only her desire to get some kind of reaction from him had led to the prank that landed them in this race. Ignoring the pain, she kept stroking. And singing. "Stroke, stroke, stroke. Paddle, paddle, paddle, *hut*." She repeated the words, adding lyrics from random songs. Childhood songs, nonsensical rhyming tunes, hymns. She paddled along, singing to herself, almost forgetting Silas rode in the boat with her. Almost.

Nat broke off mid-song, asking, "We're making good time, aren't we? We made it to the first checkpoint in four hours, despite the late start." She hesitated to mention the capsize, opting for a positive note.

Silas gave another grunt. This one leaned toward noncommittal. Finally, he spoke. "How's the pain?"

What? His tone suggested he'd been aware of it for a while. Here she thought she'd been hiding it pretty well. As she turned, he was peering at her under the brim of his cowboy hat.

She faced front again, not ready to tell him each stroke stabbed.

"It's taking a toll." The nonjudgmental words and his scratchy voice wrapped around her throbbing side, making her want to spill the entire story. Except he'd chalk it up to irresponsibility. She stiffened her back, viciously jabbing downward. Water splashed against her hot cheeks. Maybe he'd quit with the questions if she told him. She blew out a stream of air, hating the prolonged ache it produced. Opting for the bare-bones version, she said, "Last night, while riding my scooter, a deer ran me off the road."

Another grunt. This time, an acknowledgement of sorts. Her quick glimpse backward showed his chest expanding as he pulled in air, brows forming a single line across his forehead. Concern or aggravation?

Her nostrils flared. Considering her revelation, his passivity bothered her. Then he said, "I wish you'd told me back at the hotel. It needs to be looked at."

Resentment fading, she said, "No time. I hoped a good night's sleep would … fix it." Good grief. Now he'd really think she'd acted irresponsibly. Immature. Unwise. An endless list of her faults followed.

She thrust the paddle into the water, dumbfounded when he said, "I hear you. Been in situations where I had no choice other than to keep going."

His voice stretched through the relentless sunlight, touching her with its gentleness. "Still need to have it looked at, though. I brought first aid stuff."

Not much she could do about the bruises, but ointment for her arm sounded heavenly. It would alleviate her worry about the scratches getting infected and allow her to concentrate on the race.

"Just think about it, sweetheart. It's hard to watch you hurting."

Nat blinked back the moisture clouding her vision, glad for her sunglasses. A tender comment from Sy? Impatience she could have handled better.

CHAPTER TWELVE

Silas heard the partiers first. The laughing grew louder at Fentress Bridge. As the canoe swept around another tight corner, Silas spied a rainbow of colored tubes ahead. Nat had to have seen them. He shouted, "Are you feeling aggressive, or should we trade places?"

Instead of a verbal answer, Nat steered to the right toward the bank, avoiding partially submerged stumps. In knee-deep water, they jumped out to trade places, then Silas steered back into the deeper channel. She looked pale, despite the sun, but her jaw set in a determined fashion. They were of one mind. It would require extra chops to get through packs of tubers intent on partying. They wouldn't pay a whit of attention to a canoe racing down the river.

All along the private property, cabanas with drinks for sale had cropped up, drawing mounds of people. To Silas, they were human obstacles slowing them down. They had no choice except to nose the canoe through, though Silas picked up speed at any opportunity. Gradually, he formed a system of sorts. Children, he gave grace to. All other bodies just needed to get out of the way.

He passed an enormous man in stars and stripes swim trunks who paused long enough from herding teens to favor him with a dirty look. A glance back showed Nat blowing the guy a kiss. Yeah, okay. Her beauty helped counter his beastly aggression. He really didn't care about the glares or smothered curses. A yellow tube sailed past the canoe's bow, the young woman not aware it almost plowed into her. Inch by inch, they navigated, with Nat yelling *thank you* with alternating levels of grace and sarcasm, and him bullying the canoe through any narrow route within the river channel.

A prickle started up his back. The last time this had happened ... Silas tore his attention away from the river to scan the bank. A cloud moved across the sun, creating a shadow. He should be relieved for a break from the relentless glare, except the prickle morphed into a steely warning. He searched through the crowds, his focus landing on a solitary figure beside a large cabana. A man, his face hidden behind a support. As if he chose not to be seen. Silas's body tingled. The familiar stance. Military ... and something else. A tiny shard of memory surfaced, then vanished. Silas concentrated on the elusive image. The distinctive smell of gun oil rose in his consciousness.

A gun range.

"Silas," Nat called. "We going down the river or what?"

He jerked, then automatically paddled again, fighting to redirect his thoughts to the race. Getting through the tubers. The happy noise of people having a good time. He deliberately set the uneasiness aside so he could tend to the business of getting the canoe down the river.

Mile after mile, they meandered through the crowds of tubers until they thinned out. "Another boat," Silas yelled as he picked up the stroke rate. Nat worked at keeping up, however much her strokes dragged. Her needs included pain gel and a nap. Frustrated, Silas wanted to kick something, but he had to keep paddling. He'd pick up her slack as long as possible. Then what?

Lord, she needs Your help more than anything from me.

He spied the Luling Dam in the distance. "Portage ahead," he called back. Would Nat be able to lift the boat? They had to make it to the Luling checkpoint for her to receive help. She'd stayed quiet at the mention of first aid. Probably because Lacy would be the obvious choice to help. It didn't take a high IQ to understand Nat wouldn't want that. He didn't blame her. Lacy grated on him worse than Nat ever did. Any feelings he'd had for Lacy had long since disappeared. Better yet, she gave off the impression it went both ways. So why was she still here?

Silas shrugged off the question. Lacy classified as small potatoes. He still couldn't shake the feeling someone was keeping tabs on them for all the wrong reasons.

BY LATE AFTERNOON, the woods surrounding the river resembled a painting. Soft greens. A spectrum of browns. Somewhere during the afternoon, the clear water had washed into a grayish green color. A white egret stalked the shallows on the left bank, its beak poking in the water for tiny fish. Sounds of human activity carried on the wind. The hot day grudgingly gave way to lower temps.

As they rounded a slight bend, Gramps shouted, "Over here." Oh, finally. They'd reached the Luling checkpoint.

Nat clambered out of the boat, then snatched the tow handle. Silas had already jumped out, tugging the canoe beside a rocky outcropping. Nat's legs wobbled with fatigue. Silas had the first aid kit in hand. He said something to Mike, then steered her into the trees. She couldn't muster the energy to resist. He stopped by a giant fallen tree limb and pointed for her to sit on it. She sat, uncertain how to handle the situation. She needn't have worried.

"Here." He handed her a towel he'd produced from somewhere. "Take off your shirt and cover yourself with the towel. Let me know when you're decent." He turned his back to her, busying himself with the first aid box.

Nat struggled out of the snug long-sleeved sports shirt, feeling very puny. She wrapped the towel around her middle, careful to only let the straps of her sports bra show, even though she normally worked out in similar outfits … Might be time to rethink her attire if Silas's modesty posed an issue.

"All clear," she murmured.

He turned with a tube of ointment in hand. Whistling sharply, his eyes widened at the road rash on her arm. "Good grief, Nat. No wonder you've been in agony." He straddled the wide limb and dabbed antibiotic cream on the smaller scratches, then worked his way to the elongated one around her elbow. "This one needs a bandage."

Nat nodded. His light touch with the cream provided instant relief from the ongoing heat of the abrasions.

"I'll doctor the road rash. What concerns me more is the way you're moving. It might be more than simple bruises."

So he'd figured out that part too. "I'll be fine. Jesse doesn't need to know," she said testily.

Silas responded with a droll look. "It'd be better if you straight up told him."

"Promise me." She knew her insistence put him in a bad position, but she wouldn't give them a reason to pull her out of the race, no matter how badly she hurt.

He gazed at her, as if to read her soul, then shrugged. "If

you're sure, we need to get going. Please eat something." He left, his footsteps making no noise on the damp leaves.

"Thank you," she called after him.

Back on the river, they paddled the boat along the shady side as Silas navigated around the shallow gravel bars in the middle, finding the fastest currents. The brief reprieve from the sun cooled Nat's skin, even if the overhanging branches kept messing with her hat. Fear shimmied down her spine as she knocked a rather large spider away from her face. Another took its place. She batted it away, hoping this new threat wouldn't multiply. Gauzy web brushing against her made her skin crawl. They must have disturbed a nest of them.

After several rounds of *hut*, Silas called out, "Hard left." She crouched to duck under a low-hanging branch, still paddling. A sickening smack, then the boat crunched to a halt. Silas's oar shot into the water. Fortunately, it drifted alongside the boat.

Leaning out, she snatched it.

Silas had fallen backward into the boat and wasn't moving. Blood gushed from his forehead.

Her scream ripped through the hot, still air.

CHAPTER THIRTEEN

A cool wet hand kept brushing his brow. Water flowed nearby. He opened one eye, then shut it again. The heat blazed despite the shady tree. The smell of antiseptic floated on the air. When did he lay down? He struggled to rise, yet gave in when the hand pushed him back down.

"Easy there, partner. You'll upset the boat."

His eyes shot open at the soft, familiar voice. Nat stood in the water near his head. Slowly, the pieces came back. Big branch. No time to swerve. His hand touched his forehead, only to have Nat push it away.

"Don't. I cleaned the scrape, so all it needs is a bandage." She fumbled in the red first aid bag. She pulled out the supplies and doctored his head. "Not pretty, but now it won't bleed into your eye." Her lips curved into a sassy smile. "Once the swelling goes down, you'll be ruggedly handsome." She handed him a bottle of Gatorade.

Handsome? Not a category he would have picked. A severe case of teenage acne put too many pits in his face for that. To say nothing of the shrapnel scarring. He blinked, tipping the bottle into his parched mouth. The sweet-salty liquid sliding down his throat helped to clear his mind. "Thanks. Help me get upright."

Nat grasped his biceps to help him into a sitting position.

She studied him. "You took a hard knock and need to rest. That's the good news. The bad news is our ride is wedged in a tree stump."

He stared at her. "We're stuck?" The waves lapping at the boat had no rhythm. Then he spied a branch sticking through the hull. The throbbing in his head increased. In slow motion, he hopped out. Nat waded to the stern in waist-deep water. He sloshed his way to the bow. They grabbed the tow handles and attempted to slide the boat out. No soap.

"Need help?" A man sitting bow in a multi-man team called. They paddled swiftly in the river flow. Other than asking, they didn't slow their stroke rate.

Before Silas deciphered why help was a no-go, Nat sang out, "No, thanks." At her response, the TWS rules floated back into focus. Help from another team would mean instant disqualification. He waved them on, heartened by Nat's adamant refusal, glad one of them knew how much it mattered.

The men waved back. "Best of luck," one guy yelled. If a team hit a snag—literally, in their case—but still wanted to push through, it inspired other racers.

He turned back to their unyielding canoe.

"Think we can get it out in one piece?" Nat asked.

Silas glanced at the sky. Darkness would only compound the issue. "Pray, Glitter Girl. No way to win with half a boat." *Or finish.* Their watery predicament quickly countered his light words. For the next fifteen minutes, no amount of pushing, coaxing, wheedling, or cajoling moved the canoe. Finally, he unclipped the Swiss army knife from his belt loop, held his breath, and dived. He located the smallest branch holding the boat captive and hacked away. It snapped with little effort. The boat lurched forward an inch.

He surfaced, gulping air. "Help me push, Nat." His voice sounded desperate to his ears. Nat was already tugging. Together they rocked it gently.

"Woo hoo!" Nat yelled, once the boat floated free from the broken tree fingers. One arm hemming the boat, she splashed her way over, throwing her other arm around him.

Headache forgotten, he hugged her back. The celebration provided an excellent excuse to hold her tight. All too soon, she danced away. "We need to make up the lost time," she shouted.

"We've got another problem." In their haste to get the boat unsnagged, he'd forgotten about the branch poking through the hull. Now water rushed into the canoe similar to a fire hydrant on holiday.

"Oh, yikes! Now what?"

"The boat needs to dry out first, then we tape it."

"Pretty big gash. Think your Gorilla tape will hold it?" Nat asked with a worried look.

Silas's shoulders rose a fraction. "Hope so. It's all we've got."

Nat's brows knit together as she maneuvered toward the bank. "One thing's for sure. Our prayer lives are getting a workout."

Silas had the nagging feeling they'd be praying a lot more before Seadrift.

They tugged the boat up the steep bank in search of a level place.

"I'll get the tape." Nat said as they lay the injured boat on its side.

"No, we have to wait until the boat dries." He'd be the one

to apply it. Nat and heavy duty duct tape made for a dubious combo. From their perch, Silas watched a tandem canoe glide past. Their competition now had a leg up.

Nat rose, weariness etched in each body movement. "A campfire will help. I'll look for wood if you'll start the fire." A smile flickered across her lips. "Since I don't remember how."

Silas dug around in the canoe for a lighter and the tape. It would have been easier to fib, but she'd freely admitted her ignorance about building a fire. Another notch of respect hammered away at his previous disdain.

Shortly, she returned, piling a few dead sticks of wood together. He added a fuel starter. Soon, wispy spirals of fire and smoke climbed upward. Now they had nothing to do except wait for the boat to dry. Glumly, he spied another boat paddling down the river. This unscheduled stop played havoc with his patience level.

Nat broke into his musings with a somber question. "Are you willing to continue, even if we can't win?"

He shrugged, unwilling to admit defeat. "We might still catch up." He didn't want Nat to realize their chances of winning were fading by the second. "I want to continue, no matter what."

"No matter what?" Her posture, slack the moment before, straightened.

"No matter what." He affirmed, poking the fire with a broken branch.

"Good. What we need now is s'mores." Nat plopped next to him. The firelight bathed her in a warm glow. He couldn't remember why he'd ever imagined her as flighty. True, her normal bird-like movements had slowed, yet it wasn't merely physical. Mentally, she'd proven as tough as the elite soldiers he'd served with. Not a complainer either, though there were plenty of reasons to indulge.

"You eat s'mores?" Relieved for a topic they usually disagreed on, he allowed sarcasm to creep into his voice. As if to hide his changing perception of her.

"Yes. Anything with chocolate." She faced him with a sassy smile. "Surprised?"

He gave a noncommittal grunt. Drat. Another thing they had in common. He'd always had a weakness for chocolate. Chocolate milk after a hard workout. Chocolate dessert. A pair of warm chocolate eyes …

"I don't go anywhere without it." Nat proudly held up a chocolate bar, retrieved from a waterproof pocket. "Wanna share?"

"Sure." Chocolate would be most welcome, considering they were losing any previous race advantage with each passing minute.

Silas took the piece she held out. He let it melt on his tongue, savoring the silky texture. Mm. Nat had great taste in chocolate. His eyes caught hers and stayed too long.

He shifted, looking away from her. "Who taught you about campfires?"

She stared pensively into the fire. "Jesse and Rory. When they were 'tween-age,' they'd let me tag along on their campouts." Her lips firmed into a line. "They knew taking me with them was better than leaving me at home. Dad could be … unpredictable."

Silas swallowed, enjoying the last of the treat as he mulled over her words. Her bleak explanation made him grateful Gramps had stepped in. Who knew what would have happened if his mother had stayed in the picture. He got up, aching from the all-day paddle. His fingers probed around the boat's hull. At last, the surface had dried. Time for the next step.

Showing Nat how to hold the jagged edges, he taped

carefully, conserving the roll. If they ran out, the rip in the Kevlar wouldn't hold. Silas wasn't ready to call it quits over a shortage of tape.

Nocturnal creatures rustled close by, drawing a slight gasp and frown from Nat. Smiling, Silas inspected the patch one last time. "Ready to get back on the river?"

CHAPTER FOURTEEN

"Yes." Her curt tone delighted him in a way he couldn't explain. "I'll put out the fire." His grin broadened as she kicked dirt on the blaze to smother it. Things that went bump in the night threw the mighty Nat off her game.

"You want the bow?" he asked once they arrived at the water's edge. Moonlight streamed through the trees, creating an ethereal curtain. As if they were the only two people on the river, though he'd seen a constant flow of folks paddling by.

"You pick. I don't care anymore." Her simple answer arrowed straight into his heart. An appreciation stirred within him for her presence.

He headed toward the bow, giving her a reprieve from the bugs attracted to the bow lights they wore on their hats. She dove for the stern as if a little kid. Her grateful smile lifted his mood. He worked to get his seat cushion at a good angle. Then they took off.

Reinvigorated, he dug his paddle into the river as if searching for gold. The moon glow dimmed, darkening the trees to weird shadows. Bugs swarmed around his face. Good thing he had practice with long stints of motionless activity. The occasional squeaks of restlessness behind him indicated Nat wasn't faring as well.

"Silas, look." She motioned with a paddle toward an exposed gravel bar. He turned, his light casting toward a man sleeping beside his canoe. Dead to the world. "I'd be stinkin' afraid to sleep on a gravel bar. Not with critters on the loose."

"He's too exhausted to care." Silas could relate, though Nat didn't need to know. Lightheadedness had replaced his headache. He didn't know if it sprang from his depleted energy level or if the bang to his head had entered a new stage. Surely, it hadn't been hard enough to cause a concussion. As long as he kept paddling, it wasn't so bad.

"How're you doing?" He stayed forward, knowing the words would carry back to her.

"I'm good. You?"

"I'm good." He tamped down a swell of anxiousness. It seemed as if another crisis waited around the corner.

She paused, then said, "This isn't what I expected." Another pause. "You're not what I expected."

The velvety night air, still humid, blanketed him. "Ditto. You've got"—he hem-hawed—"pluck." Inwardly cringing, he hoped she wouldn't throw her oar at him.

"Yeah, you've been a good partner too," she said softly. A pause followed, then she asked, "Let's play the question game."

That sounded ... intrusive. "Mm. I'm not usually into a bunch of questions."

Her amused laugh spilled toward him. "Nobody besides you and me on this stretch of river, bud. I'm good at keeping secrets."

Secrets? Nat? She struck him as an open book. Unless she wore a certain look. He shook off the niggling idea he didn't have a clue about this woman. It was still better she didn't know certain things about him.

"What if we promise to tell the truth, even if the answer is 'I don't want to talk about it.'"

He hoped she wouldn't get mad when he took her up on it.

IT TOOK EONS, but the pain relievers had kicked in. Nat worked to banish self-consciousness about her bedraggled appearance. They had been paddling a canoe with no sleep. Any attempt to spruce up would be pure vanity. After a stern internal conversation with her mewling flesh about priorities, she captured self-pitying thoughts in favor of the greater good. Getting this race behind them ranked more important than hair or makeup.

Glad for the darkness, she concentrated on what she wanted to know most about Mr. Mysterious. Best start with the harmless questions he'd answer. "You're a vet, same as Jesse?"

"Yep."

"What did you do? Your specialty? Been a while, so I'm fuzzy on correct terminology." Nat's oar swished through the water with purpose.

His answer came slowly. "I was a sniper." The square set of his shoulders had slumped.

Oh, dear. No wonder the man used words sparsely. He'd probably seen, had to do things she couldn't imagine. Tread carefully, girl. "How did that happen? I mean, did they pick you or what?" His guarded response suggested he'd choose differently now.

Once she'd decided he wouldn't answer, he gave an indifferent shrug. "I had good aim. Climbed through the levels.

When I reached sharpshooter, they asked if I wanted sniper training."

Crickets sang an off-tune melody in the trees as Nat chewed on his response. "I take it you wanted to?"

"It was the cool option." The cricket song grew louder. "So I stuffed down my desire to be a medic. Decided to kill people instead of heal them." Regret sliced through the words.

Nat inhaled a sharp breath, trying not to overreact. "Hm. I think you're being hard on yourself. You were in a war. What about the people you saved? I know you've heard it before because Pastor Mike says it all the time. God's forgiveness covers everything, not just the elementary stuff."

He paddled so fast, she struggled to keep up. "You know you're forgiven, right?" she persisted. He needed to understand the unending grace of forgiveness. For his sake.

"I know," he said. They paddled in silence. "My turn to ask you questions."

Nat's paddle swished quietly through the water. The sweet chocolate-y aftertaste turned sour in her mouth. Not a good sign. *C'mon, cowboy. Help get my mind off how wretched I feel.*

Silas cleared his throat. "Why self-defense seminars? Aside from being good at them, people usually have reasons for what they do."

Not her favorite subject, yet the soft darkness somehow made it easier to talk about. "Growing up, Dad's alcoholism affected our home life. Mom caught the brunt of it. Enough for me to realize I never wanted to be in her shoes. So I learned how to defend myself. From there, it grew into helping other women learn to do the same."

Silas stoked steadily, not offering any response. Not an awkward silence, though. She'd learned his way of processing things. Small splashes nearby indicated fish in the area.

Keeping up with his stroke rate, she watched tiny pools of water grow wider.

"So, have you had to use your skills?"

At her lack of answer, he asked, "Is that a no or I-don't-want-to-talk-about-it?"

"Once," Nat admitted.

"Did he back off?"

"Mostly." Colin didn't understand *no*. He pretended her pushing him away didn't bother him, but she knew it wouldn't last. Another reason for her hasty exit out of the relationship.

"It was the guy you were hanging out with a month ago."

"That's not a question." Tartness crept into her voice. She thrust her paddle into the water with more force than necessary.

He went on as if she hadn't responded. "He wasn't your type."

"Who's my type, Mr. Romance Guru?"

His easy shrug showed no offense. "Not him."

They paddled in silence for a while until Nat spoke up again. "Who's your type? Lacy?"

He grunted. "We're only friends. I'm not interested in more."

"As in, not with her or not at all?"

He steered around a cluster of stumps. "Probably the latter."

"Why?"

Instead of answering, he slapped around his face. "Persistent bugs." Blowing out an extended breath, he said, "I'm one of those guys with a boatload of baggage and no desire to talk about it."

Nat mulled over this new revelation. Silas rarely talked about anything. This canoe ride had brought more words out of him than in all the time she'd known him.

Her eyelids kept sliding shut, given the hypnotic darkness, though her hands pushed the paddle. Desperate to keep her eyes open, she sang another chorus of "Amazing Grace." Silas joined in, his raspy voice scrapping at the tune as if his throat needed perpetual clearing.

The bank beckoned her. If she could just rest her body for a few minutes … "Silas, I need a break. Aren't we about to Palmetto? I need to lie down a bit …"

"Take a NoDoz. We're still making up for the slow start. No stopping at the checkpoint. I've already arranged it with Mike. We're only going to slow down enough to get fresh water jugs."

Tears welled up. He couldn't be so heartless. She dug around for the plastic container of meds. Finally, she located the small bottle and slipped two caplets into her mouth. Picking up the oar again, she found the familiar rhythm. Stroke. Swish. Stroke.

"Just keep paddling, Nat."

A brief nap sounded lovely, apart from knowing if they stopped, she'd be hard-pressed to get back in the boat, and they might not finish. Silas knew it too. Neither of them wanted a DNF emblazoned across their entry. Faint gratefulness for his superior strength stirred deep down.

Once the Palmetto checkpoint appeared, they exchanged the jugs without a word. Mike waved them on, his lips tightly pressed together. Her heart warmed a tad with the human contact, however short-lived. Inky black darkness relieved by the moon and stars between enormous tree limbs. The occasional fish splashed. Night birds called. The soft swish of their paddles in the water.

Amid stomach cramps, she said, "Sing to me." Wrong way to ask for help, except she no longer cared about a trivial word slip.

Thankfully, he had no sharp comeback. His voice lifted over her tummy pain. He sang a few words from "You and Me," a song made popular by Lighthouse. The rough warbles gained traction. He branched into other songs until it almost seemed he'd forgotten her presence. His rusty medley of sweet love tunes interspersed with worship songs drifted over the foggy river. Eerie. Haunting. After he finished a particular song, he'd harken back to the "You and Me" lyrics.

She joined him, singing along with the ones she recognized. The caffeine pills, i.e., the NoDoz, took effect, helping to curb the drowsiness, exclusive of her colicky stomach. She tore open a Gu and squirted the energy gel down her throat. It would have to do until the next checkpoint.

Not often enough, they passed another canoe. Other paddlers sat on the banks, staring into a campfire, the lines in their faces hard. She said quiet prayers for them as she and Silas passed. Nat didn't mention stopping again. It would only make things worse. If only her stomach would cooperate.

CHAPTER FIFTEEN

Silas glanced up at the starry night again as a distraction from the ever-present bugs. They had to keep going, though his hands ached something fierce. If only the dratted current would pick up. Inching down the river hadn't been the plan. He checked his watch for the umpteenth time. He'd noticed another couple on the bank about a half mile back. Hands on hips, the woman glared at her male partner. Other than them, he'd seen no other tandem boats since yesterday. He knew from registration there were others on the river. In this arduous race, miles would pass without seeing a soul.

The competitive urge nagged at him. *Lord, you know how much I obsess about winning.* Was the event meant as a tempering cauldron? The desire to smoke the competition remained, except for Nat. Silas didn't know if he'd lost his grip or if wisdom had finally taken hold. For her sake, he'd slowed the pace. He couldn't yell at her to stroke faster when she was in obvious pain.

Yep. He was drowning in all things Nat.

As she sat in the bow, his eyes stayed glued to her slim

back. He'd memorized the way she paddled. Knew the exact moments her side ached. The way her ponytail caught up in her hat, his fingers itched to comb through it.

Without warning, Nat stopped paddling. Then she retched over the side of the boat. He knocked aside his first reaction. Anger, even if based in frustration, wouldn't help matters. Slowly, compassion took over. She tried so hard to be brave. The Nat he knew wouldn't throw up in front of anyone, let alone him. What could possibly reside in her stomach? The woman had eaten next to nothing all day. Must be the nasty Gu junk.

Silas steered the boat toward the bank, then holed up under an overhanging tree. He'd manage some privacy just in case someone happened by. The retching sounds continued. He eased into the water to get closer to her, careful not to upend the canoe. She sat limply, head resting on her arms against the gunnel.

"Don't come closer," she croaked. "I stink."

"I've smelled worse," he retorted, as he dug his feet into the soft silt of the riverbed. "You're shivering. Lean back into my arms so you can warm up."

With unNat-like sluggishness, she rested her head against his damp chest. "I don't know if I'm done." She leaned forward, rinsing her mouth with water from a jug, then spit over the side.

He encased his arms around her, whispering against her ear. "I can wait it out, sweetheart." He bit his tongue not to unleash any more endearments.

"I'm slowing you down." The last word eclipsed on a sob.

It came so naturally to lay his cheek next to hers. "I'm sorry you got sick. I forgot you hadn't eaten much. NoDoz is brutal on an empty stomach."

Her jaw dropped. "That'll teach you to boss me around."

"Yes, ma'am." Surprisingly content, he rubbed her arms, then held her. Streaking down the river to win a medal had completely lost its charm. His eyes shut.

He didn't know how much time had passed. *Not long enough.* He still stood in the river, holding Nat. Leaning into her, he said, "Stomach settled enough to paddle?"

She opened her eyes. Wearily, she grabbed her paddle, then laid it aside. Filling her cowboy hat with river water, she tipped it onto her head. Water streamed down her hair and face.

He adjusted his cowboy hat tighter. "Nice way to cool off."

She squinted at him. "Good way to get rid of the puke smell."

He couldn't help grinning.

A dainty blush stained her cheeks. Her lips stretched in the first smile he'd seen in miles. "What happens on the river—"

"Stays on the river. Your secret's safe with me." He hated they had no choice except to continue. Reluctantly, he moved toward the stern. The sooner they got this race over with, the sooner Nat would recover.

RARELY WAS Silas so glad to see a sunrise. Pinkish streaks shot through a cerulean sky. As they coasted into the Gonzales checkpoint, Silas needed a brief break from paddling. Nat needed one too.

"What happened?" Lacy stood, arms crossed. She stared at Silas's forehead as he ran the canoe onto the pebbled bank.

"Argument with a tree." As Lacy reached for the bandage, he batted her hand away. "I'm fine. Hungry. You brought food, Gramps?"

"It still needs checking out. You might have a concussion, Silas." Lacy stood her ground. Silas took the pizza box.

"Did you hear the latest, Sy? Another tandem canoe made the checkpoint about thirty minutes ago." Nat came from where she'd been talking to Mike. Her eyes found the pizza box. "Does it have sausage?"

"It's got the works. Pick off what you don't want. Put it on mine," Silas said around a mouthful. He held out his piece.

She gave him a small smile. "My sausage for your mushrooms?"

He nodded. Using their fingers, they traded toppings. He chuckled at Lacy's eye roll. Exchanging pizza ingredients struck him as minor, considering their previous level of closeness. He watched Nat take a huge bite. She chewed as if famished.

Eyes widening, he asked, "You're hungry?"

She shrugged, her mouth full.

Pastor Mike held up a thermos. "Coffee?"

"Half a cup," Nat said.

"Same for me," Silas said.

Lacy intervened with a frown. "You shouldn't have a stimulant."

"I said I'm fine, Lace." Silas accepted the Styrofoam cup of dark brew.

"I'll keep an eye on him." The smallest of smirks hovered around Nat's mouth.

Silas tingled with warmth that had nothing to do with the rising sun. "Back to the boat?"

Lacy huffed, plopping into a folding chair with her arms crossed. Gramps gazed at Silas, a mix of empathy and longing in his eyes. "I'd spell you if they'd let me, Sy."

"You'd do it in a heartbeat, I know." Gramps had always been in his corner. His unflagging support served as the grounding rod Silas had desperately needed in his younger years. A surreal feeling had stolen over him. After twenty-four hours plus of paddling, he'd discovered a new concept. One he suspected Nat had known all along. The canoe race had little to do with who reached the finish line first. It was more about discovering a person's true character. The hidden part that God saw so clearly. Getting his perspective realigned had become the real win.

Nat lobbed a tiny package his way. He caught it easily, then examined the contents. "Way to go, Nat. Toothbrush with toothpaste. All the comforts of home." He tore it open and popped the toothbrush in his mouth. Lacy appeared by his side. She peered at the palms of his hands, then pulled out her ever-present phone for pictures.

Chugging the rest of her shake, Nat swallowed more pain meds.

He nodded toward the canoe. "You ready to get back in our thunder boat?"

Confusion wrinkled her brow. "What's a thunder boat?"

"Those go-fast babies that hydroplane across the water. It's what we need to catch up." He climbed into the stern. Nat slid into the bow with the help of a stout tree branch.

"Don't know about you, but I'm ready for this race to end," Nat sighed.

"Me too, sweetheart." Silas hoped Nat hadn't noticed his repeated use of the affectionate term. Paddling twenty-four hours with one tiny nap, surely, she wouldn't hold him responsible for anything he said. Emotionally, they both teetered on the edge.

Silas had full control of the stern. His heart remained an entirely different matter.

CHAPTER SIXTEEN

Nat adjusted her cowboy hat. By tacit agreement, they'd eased up on hard questions. It was requiring all their brain power to not fall into a stupor. Her eyeballs resembled river bottom gravel. The simple act of dragging her paddle out of the water for another stroke had become a challenge.

She gazed at her feet. Oh, no. "Silas, the boat is taking on water."

"I know. The bilge pump isn't working right. I'll tinker with it at Cheapside."

Worst-case scenarios popped into Nat's mind. What if they couldn't fix it? What if they couldn't finish? The what-ifs pounded away without mercy. Nat jerked to attention once she realized where her headspace landed. She shouted, "Whatever things are true, whatever things are honorable, whatever things are right, whatever things are pure"—she wound down —"that's all I can remember."

"Think on these things. Not negative stuff. We need to focus on finishing instead of all the reasons we can't."

"What if we can't fix the bilge pump?"

"We got this, sweetheart. Just keep paddling. We're almost at the checkpoint," Silas said.

The scent of barbecue floated toward them. Familiar voices cheered.

Warm tears rolled down Nat's cheeks. Mercy, she was a total wreck. Without a word, they hauled the boat onto a grassy patch on the bank. His warm hand gripped her shoulder. "I got this. Eat something, then lay down. Catch a few winks."

It had been several hours since she'd eaten, but food had no appeal. Sleep, however, beckoned her with dreamy fingers. Jesse had come up behind Silas, brows knotted. Because of her appearance, no doubt. If she looked anywhere as awful as she felt, his alarm was justified. Once Rory appeared, no amount of blinking could hide her tears. He'd acted as her second brother for years. An excellent advocate when Jesse got too stuffy. Occasional partner-in-crime.

Pastor Mike handed her a container filled with a protein drink, then stood by with an avocado. Once she'd slaked her thirst, she took half of the avocado and spooned a bite into her mouth. The creamy green fruit slid down her throat. She chased it with the dregs of her drink. Mike offered her a small portion of a sandwich. Wanting to ease his worried look, she took it. The meaty brisket smell tickled her nose. Too bad her stomach rebelled.

Facing away from Mike, Nat fed Elvis the sandwich, paying no attention to Silas's "rule." Silas gestured to Rory with the roll of Gorilla tape. Her lips twitched. All serious boaters carried the sticky adhesive. Silas explaining its role to Rory made perfect sense. For all Rory's good looks and business smarts, the man stayed a total doofus about fixing things.

Silas walked toward her, Rory on his heels. A smile creased

Silas's sunburned cheeks. "I fixed the pump. A wire had, um, disengaged."

"What made it disengage?" Nat asked. If it happened once, it would happen again. Next time, they might not be in a good place to repair it.

"Probably when the boat got stuck in the tree. The all-day paddling clinched it." He favored her with his trademark half-smirk. Somewhere in this endless ride, it had stopped irritating her.

Merely an endearing trait.

"Hello, Nat." Rory smiled, looking dapper as ever with a polo shirt tucked into a pair of light-weight jeans. "Vi wanted to give you massages, except Jesse said it would be against the rules."

Nat gave him a tired smile. "I would have loved her hands on me." Vi wasn't only a good friend, she stayed a much-sought-after massage therapist at Peeps. "How's she doing?"

"Absolutely fantastic." He beamed from ear to ear. A few weeks ago, they'd announced her pregnancy with twins. "Between the blazing heat and doctor's order to rest, I convinced her to stay home."

"Bet that went over well."

"About like you'd imagine." The words leaked with affection as Rory's gaze moved behind her.

Silas's breath tickled her ear. "The no-physical-touch-rule doesn't apply to partners."

Slow to grasp his meaning, Nat felt his hands on her shoulders, rubbing her sore muscles. A protest formed on her lips, then died as his thumbs massaged one knot after another. She shut her eyes at Rory's knowing smile. Best to enjoy the moment without complications.

All too soon, it stopped. Rolling her neck, she appreciated the increase in mobility. "Vi's got serious competition. Thank you." The words were inadequate compared to his attentiveness. She turned to face him, realizing too late his soft eyes would be her undoing. Unable to resist, she kissed him. Just a sweet smooch to convey her gratefulness. He stiffened with surprise.

They stepped apart as if nothing happened when Lacy sauntered over, clipboard in hand. "Y'all are actually making excellent time, despite the setbacks." She stared at the dirty bandage on Silas's forehead and gave Nat a look of blame. "You still might not finish. Forty teams have already dropped out, you know."

Was she crazy? Silas's eyes had narrowed. Determination set his jaw.

"Lace, we've paddled one hundred forty-seven miles in forty-eight hours. Quitting is not an option," he said. Ouch. Nary an ounce of softness or diplomacy.

It had its desired effect, though, because Lacy stepped back, raising her hands in surrender. "Okay, I hear you." She handed the clipboard to Gramps. "You're doing great. I'm just saying—"

Silas swiveled away from her. His hand found the small of Nat's back, nudging her forward. "Let's do this."

Alrighty, then.

TWENTY-OR-SO MILES LATER, Silas couldn't shake the ever-increasing uneasiness. He swiped another insect away from his face. Stings and bites no longer mattered. Nat remained steady, though the set of her slim shoulders spelled fatigue. She'd had no argument when he took the bowman position.

He scanned the thin tree lines, a sniper habit he hadn't

used in a while. The sixth sense he'd developed on missions had niggled at him for the last thirty minutes. Tricks of a tired mind? So far, he'd spied nothing. The bustle of the upper river had kept him alert. These lengthy, isolated stretches were in cahoots with a dose of Ambien.

Fish flipped out of the water, silver flashes in the relentless sunshine. Normally, he soaked in the peaceful sounds. Now he envied their energy.

The wind had picked up, cooling the blazing heat. Clouds shadow-danced across the sun. A soft shower might lull him out of this hazy lassitude.

Something in his peripheral vision made him scan the tree line again. There. A telltale glint poked through leafy branches. A gun aimed their way. Too late, he heard a shot.

Nat's pink flag exploded.

"Over and under!" He jerked the side so hard, they both dumped into the water. He thrashed around, grabbing for a hold of the capsized canoe.

Nat surfaced, spluttering water. "What—"

He yanked her under the boat, transferring his grip to the other side. "Hold it here." As she reached, he lowered it into her hands, then stepped behind her, shielding her with his body.

Ping. Ping. Ping. Gunshots plinked around the canoe. He crouched to keep the boat level with the water line, so their movements were undetectable.

"What's happening?" Nat asked. Confusion threaded through the words.

He put a finger to his lips. "Wait till I give an all-clear."

They waited. Silas desperately wanted a peek at the shooter, except he couldn't leave Nat unprotected.

Fifteen minutes passed. He motioned for her to wade toward the opposite bank. He followed, keeping the boat aloft to provide a modicum of protection.

Once they reached the bank, he peered out, spotting a rocky ledge nearby. "I want you to take cover behind those rocks. Do it quickly."

"What about you?" Her eyes were enormous orbs of fear.

"I'm going to heft the boat around to distract him." Silas would know quickly if the guy meant business.

They executed his hastily devised plan. Nat scuttled down behind the rocks. Silas suspected the shooter had vanished once the gunfire ceased.

No trace of Nat's girl power flag remained, though eventually, some bits might float to the surface. *If* such remnants existed. As Silas stared at the empty hook, pieces fell into place. Someone watching them the day it hailed. The familiar stance of the shadowy guy in the party crowd. Faint recollections of a gun range.

Fury mounting, Silas stomped over to the wide rocky crevasse where Nat had hidden. He crawled in beside her. "Why would someone shoot at us?"

CHAPTER SEVENTEEN

Fear sliced into Nat's burned-out brain, shutting down any rational thought. "What?"

"I need answers, Nat."

"I don't know." What slammed into her brain couldn't be true. Could it?

Silas leaned until he was inches away from her face. "Level with me, Nat. I can't protect you if I'm in the dark. Who wants to scare you enough to shoot at us?"

She stared at him. "What if *you're* the one they're after?"

He shook his head. "Nobody after me would shoot your flag."

Oh.

Nat stalled, still hoping for a different conclusion.

Silas's dark eyes bored through her.

"Jesse doesn't know." Now why did those words pop out? As if her older brother had dibs on her personal life.

"Tell me what Jesse doesn't know."

"Colin." Nat whispered.

Confusion darted across Silas's craggy features, then he asked, "Your ex-boyfriend? Why?"

"I doubt Colin was the shooter. He's the type to give orders."

The line between Silas's brows deepened. "You haven't answered my question. Why would he send you a warning?" He moved closer. "He's not messing around, Natalie. What do you know about him?"

Silas knew her full name? When he said it in his low scratchy voice, she couldn't hold back. "He's a drug dealer. I never let on I knew." She brushed away the tear sliding down her cheek. "He's kind of paranoid."

Silas leaned his back against the unyielding rock. "Yeah, I bet. Illegal activities make people look over their shoulders. The bright side, if there is one, is the hitman only wanted to scare you."

Nat's shoulders slumped. "How do you know?"

Steel edged his voice. "Pretty sure I know the guy who blew away your flag. If he meant to kill you, you'd be dead. Me too."

Nat's protein drink curdled in her stomach. "What do we do now?"

"We need to tell the authorities for your sake," he said. The words belied his expression.

She studied him. "But you don't think it's a good idea."

"No evidence. The shot destroyed the flag so we can't prove anything."

"Why wouldn't they believe us?"

"For all they know, in our sleep-deprived state, we imagined the whole thing."

"It happened," Nat declared. "What about the race? Will we get to finish?" It killed her to think they'd come this far to be derailed by her vengeful ex. "You called it a warning shot, right? Do you think he'll be back?"

"Not today or soon. He wanted to scare you into keeping your mouth shut. But if Colin is paranoid, his demons won't let go until ..."

What he left unsaid chilled Nat to the bone. She swept an arm around. "No cell reception. The only thing to do is keep going for now."

"If you want to stay here, they'll track our GPS signal. Even if we don't signal for help, someone will eventually come to make sure we're okay."

Despite Silas's assurance the guy had vanished, the role of sitting duck didn't set well. Hands on hips, she asked, "What do you want to do?"

He shook his head. "Not my call."

"If you weren't concerned about protecting me, what would you do?"

"I'd keep paddling." His hazel eyes weighed her response.

She rose in one fluid motion, albeit slowly, and picked her way out of the crevasse.

"Where are you going?"

"To see if our boat is race-ready. Are you coming or not?"

He hustled next to her. "Are you sure? Your brother—"

Her eyes found his chapped, dry lips. So close, a tiny scar manifested. Her fingers itched to explore it. What she wouldn't give for a sweet, comforting kiss. The small taste she'd stolen hadn't been enough. She tore her gaze away. "I can handle Jesse."

SILAS KEPT a sharp lookout as they paddled toward the Cuero checkpoint. It couldn't come fast enough to suit him, no matter if his theory about the shooter had proved valid. No spidey sense tingling. His uneasiness had fled. Except for the shooter, it was just another day on the river. Hot. Beautiful. An irresistible mystery. Which also described the woman in the boat with him. He'd wanted to kiss her so badly, his insides pooled with frustration.

As they paddled, he'd leaned deeply into prayer, intent on hearing what the Lord had to say about their less-than-thrilling situation. All on her own, Nat started praying out loud. Her loud spontaneous prayers gave Silas goosebumps. Her chats with God matched the way she talked to everyone else. Smart. Sassy. Wildly repentant. And so endearing, he never wanted it to stop.

"How you doing up there?" He called once her entreaties to heaven had slowed.

"I'm good. Prayer keeps me from imagining things." Once again, she skimmed her cowboy hat into the water, then poured it over her head. "Is it hot enough for ya?"

With no conscious thought, he copied Nat, enjoying the brief cool splash on his head and face. He rubbed a palm against his sunglass lenses to see again. This extreme ride was choking the life out of his want-to, challenging him to the core.

"What's our plan at Cuero? Are we going to inform whoever, um … about my flag?"

Nice way of *not* saying how much danger they'd been in. "Depends on who's there."

"I'm thinking the sooner we let the authorities know, the better."

Since it wasn't a question, he didn't answer. At best, it posed a dilemma. They'd face questioning, possibly for hours. It'd also signal the end of their race. Their future at Peeps would hang in the balance. Yet, if they stayed mum and kept going, he'd never forgive himself if something happened to Nat.

Minutes later, they glided into the Cuero checkpoint. Silas

immediately noticed two things. Gramps' skin had developed an odd gray color, as if he'd been the one paddling for days. Hardly anyone else was around. Pastor Mike hurried to switch their water jugs for fresh ones. The race official had noted their arrival. He sat in a lawn chair, scribbling their time on a clipboard.

"Where's Lacy?" She'd made all the daytime checkpoints so far.

"She got a call. Said she had to go into town. She'll meet us in Valiant."

Given Nat's knowing look, Lacy was probably still miffed over his harsh words at Cheapside. "Developing a better bedside manner" had been Nat's tactful way of addressing it during one of their endless conversations. Every single thought or action during this race became fodder for discussion. They were worse than an old married couple.

Was this a microcosm of how their lives would look as a couple? Easy conversations. Challenges tempered by their mutual love for God. In perfect sync, paddling together down an endless river.

The bright thought blinded him more than the relentless sun.

"There's food if you're hungry." Words from their Team Captain broke into his reverie. "Cold pizza or barbeque sandwiches. Both in the cooler." Mike raised his voice in Nat's direction. "Plenty of avocadoes left."

Silas shook his head, making his way to where Nat stood on the muddy riverbank.

"We need to keep going, don't we?" she asked.

"Only if you're good with it."

Her eyes said she understood. Whether they continued had become her decision. "We've prayed. You'll tell me if you get bad vibes?"

He nodded. He'd also rearrange the heavens if it would make her feel better about their unique situation.

"What's ahead, Sy?" The soft question had him leaning toward her.

Somewhere along the river, she'd wrangled promises they'd always tell each other the truth. A sigh escaped his lips. "You up for an all-night paddle? We'll reach Valiant by morning." He wouldn't blame her if she wanted to quit. His aching body and fuzzy brain begged for a reprieve, except later he'd regret it. She would too.

She paused so long, he expected her to say no. Then her chin went up. Her eyes flashed fire. "Okay. Back in the boat. Valiant, here we come."

It had been so long since a woman had looked at him with trust, it became a monumental task *not* to scoop her up in his arms and carry her off to their special place. If it existed.

A narrow tippy canoe would have to do until then.

CHAPTER EIGHTEEN

Nat tended not to enjoy sunrises, mostly because of her night-owl habits. This one, however, fell into the all-together-worth-it category. Magnificent orange streaks crenellated the pearly gray sky as they paddled to the Valiant checkpoint.

"What's your favorite thing to do, Nat?" Silas sat in the bow.

Nat missed the question game last night. Aside from conserving energy, she desperately desired to stave off the experience shared by veteran racers—hallucinations. Lightheaded from lack of sleep, it took a moment for her brain to function past paddle strokes. "Despite the accident, I still enjoy riding my scooter. And paddling." *With you.*

"You're brave. If I'd taken the spill you did, don't know that I'd be keen on riding for a while."

Considering this fresh trouble, her accident appeared ancient history. *What if it wasn't?* She tucked the unwelcome thought away to ponder later. If she remembered. "So, what's *your* favorite thing?" Her keen need-to-know bordered on obsession with all-things-Silas. She dipped her oar in the shiny water. In. Out. Repeat. In. Out. Repeat.

"This paddling gig is pretty cool." His wry expression confirmed the next words. "Though it will be awhile before I'm ready to get in another boat."

"You think?" Her laugh sounded slightly hysterical.

"Thinking about getting a motorcycle. We could ride together." Silas continued looking forward, paddling as if he hadn't just dropped a bombshell into her world.

Nat swallowed back her shock. He wanted to ride with her? She answered, striving for nonchalance. "Depends. My scooter is small. You buy some big monster machine, I won't be able to keep up."

He looked back, his smile enigmatic. "You'll keep up, Glitter Girl."

She kept her blade going, mulling over his response. The gruffness she knew how to manage. He and Jesse were two peas in a pod for barking orders. Except Silas sounded almost tender. As if he yearned for more than the two of them paddling on opposite ends of a boat.

"O happy day, I see the bridge. And"—he leaned forward for a closer look— "Tavo's there."

Nat's heart thumped in loud relief. She'd hoped their cop friend would show at a checkpoint. "Is he a good one to tell about … the incident?"

"Yeah. If he doesn't roast my bacon for staying on the river."

Nat frowned. As if they'd had tons of opportunity to spill their guts. "We'll do it together."

"I got this, Nat."

Undeterred by Silas's growl, she announced with a pertness she certainly didn't feel. "If Colin is at the bottom of this, then it's my problem too."

Silas made a noise under his breath, then got out of the canoe to tug it across a shallow bar. Nat climbed out to help. Elvis greeted them, white tail moving back and forth, a king waving to his subjects.

She snatched the cold smoothie Mike handed her, then hiked over to Tavo, arriving as Silas greeted him. Ignoring Silas's exasperated look, she spoke, "Something happened."

"Hello to you too, Nat." Tavo's cheeks creased as he smiled down at her. Years ago, she'd decided God gave him dimples to offset his intimidating size. Tavo won the contest for the biggest man she'd ever seen. Jesse measured in at six-feet, two-inches, but Tavo had him beat. Probably came in handy as a police officer. Criminals would think twice before trying something. Their news wouldn't thrill him. However, she'd much rather explain to a friend than a stranger.

"What happened?" Tavo's question brought her back around.

Silas's brow arched at her. "Someone shot at our canoe."

As Tavo's eyes narrowed into slits, Nat confirmed it with a nod. "Let's go somewhere quiet." His authoritative manner had taken over.

They moved closer to his patrol car. No one disturbed them as they explained the shooting incident as best they could. It happened so fast, there wasn't much to tell aside from their suspicions. When Nat faltered with Colin's potential role, Tavo's pointed questions helped, despite the pain in her heart.

Colin wasn't a wise choice for a long-term relationship. The few times he'd let go of his sophisticated façade, she'd glimpsed an insecurity mirroring her own—probably what drew her to him. However, his "business" scared her. The values driving him weren't conducive to a happy life. She'd had to get out.

Only now, she'd become a threat. She tuned back in as the two men wrapped up their conversation.

"From what I hear about the TWS, you're headed into the most harrowing part. Sure you don't want to bow out, now that you've been targeted? A canoe race isn't the best place to ward off mischief." His gaze centered on Nat. "And you're sleep-deprived."

"Even though there's no proof or evidence, you're playing with fire. If Colin's the one behind the shots, he won't stop." His look pierced Nat. "What you've shared helps. He's been under investigation for a while. The guy's good at not getting caught." Tavo touched her chin with his thumb and forefinger. "Stay alert, Sis. We need you."

A shiver rose up her spine at the solemn look on Tavo's face. His admonishment eerily echoed Silas's take on the situation.

As she pondered Tavo's words, Silas made grating noises, as if clearing mud from his throat. "I think we're safe. No sniper in his right mind would follow us into the cuts. Too hard to follow. Easy to get lost."

"And you know this how?" Tavo asked.

Nat winced at the faint sarcasm. Apart from her, Silas answered easily. "I'm a Special Ops vet. And Nat and I have done practice runs in the cuts."

"Good to know." Tavo didn't seem put off by the pointed answer. If anything, his steady gaze held relief. "You're certain a sniper fired the shots?"

"Yeah. I've seen the guy before." Silas had Tavo's undivided attention. "He showed up at the gun range several months back."

"You get a name?"

"No. Any description of him will fit a million guys. He'll

have gone to ground and won't surface around these parts again."

"How so?"

"The set-up smells as if it's a gun-for-hire. He toyed with us, but destroying Nat's flag made it personal. Someone sent her a message."

Nat shivered despite the warm morning. Silas slid his arm around her. His solid embrace helped to tame her mounting fear. "You ready to paddle, Nat?"

As they walked toward the canoe, Silas asked with a tartness she hadn't heard before. "Why did he call you Sis?"

She lifted her shoulders, then let them drop, releasing a breath. "He and Rory stayed so tight with Jesse throughout school. I suppose I'm still the bratty little sister who tags along."

Silas came to a halt beside her, pulling her to a stop. He took her hands. Twining his fingers through hers, he said, "For what it's worth, you've been an excellent partner." His molten gaze made her knees wobbly. "I don't think of you as anybody's little sister."

Turning her to face the river, his arm caressed her shoulders. Filthy as they both were, he whispered sweet encouragement in her ear as they walked the short distance to the canoe.

His comfort had become the warm, safe place she longed for.

Before they climbed in the canoe, Lacy flounced over. Oh, dear. Her pinched countenance forecast a new slew of dire predictions.

Hands over brows to protect her eyes from the rising sun, she said saucily. "You two look beat. I hear it's only going to get worse from here on out. Why don't you quit while you're ahead?"

As Silas's mouth tightened, she added, "Gramps isn't doing so well, Sy. Have you even checked on him?"

Nat glanced at the truck where the older man stood. Without a word, Silas strode over to him. She stayed at water's edge, not knowing what to make of Lacy or her latest news about Gramps. Was this part of the woman's ongoing ploy to get them to quit the race? To what end? It puzzled Nat. Silas mentioned Gramps hadn't been his chipper self at the last checkpoint. Once Pastor Mike joined their discussion, Nat sighed with relief. The man had already proved himself tactful and solution-oriented. He'd offer the insight needed to move things along.

Despite the no-physical-contact rule, Silas gave Gramps a brief hug, then headed her way. Lacy still gave off an anxious vibe, verging on manic.

"You ready to paddle?" Silas paused to squeeze her shoulder. Nat leaned into him for several moments, then climbed into the canoe. She consigned her uncharitable thoughts about Lacy to the nether regions of her mind. Settling into the bow position, a visceral ache took hold at the empty hook where her girl power flag had flown.

Lord, help get me down this river. If Colin's behind this, please stop him.

Again, Nat pushed her rising fears away. She sneaked a peek at Silas, then slid her paddle into the golden water. Proximity forced them apart when they were in the canoe, yet she'd never felt closer.

Yes, indeed. Today was shaping up as a fine day to be on the river.

CHAPTER NINETEEN

Nat angled her paddle over her head. She grabbed both ends to stretch her arms from side to side. Her mental acuity was fading faster than she could hold on. Since morning, they'd paddled through the Coleto River confluence. She marveled at the way the rivers merged. Rushing water flowed, helping to carry them along. Keeping the canoe on an even keel trumped any saved paddle strokes. Now they were passing river houses on stilts. A welcome change from the forest-like conditions they'd traveled for miles.

"Getting close to the next checkpoint," Silas called back.

Nat peered at the bank. "Jess and Rory brought Paige. It'll be good to see another woman."

"Your brother's helping boost your morale."

"It's working." Excited barking filled the peaceful scene as Elvis waded toward them. "Look. Our canine greeting committee." Nat stared at the big plastic sheet sign. "TWS, CP 9, Swinging Bridge, mile 231. Woo hoo!" She swung legs made of lead over the canoe side. Every exit took longer.

Silas put one leg out, then the other, also moving like a

turtle. Elvis fawned all over him. His beautiful white coat shook water everywhere.

A grin on his face, Silas slapped Rory's outstretched hand. Paige hurried to enclose Nat in a hug. Despite her diminutive size, Paige rivaled any grandmother for showing affection.

Nat made her way to the beverage cooler and pulled out a Powerade. The sweet liquid slid down her throat. Instantly, she became more alert. She propped against Jesse's Jeep, sipping the drink, happy for the warm metal to hold her up.

Silas came, unwrapping a giant cheeseburger. He stood so close, the charred beef aroma enveloped her. "Take a bite."

She opened her mouth wide to chomp off a bite. "Hm. Juicy. One more," she mumbled around the mouthful.

After another bite, she waved it away. Silas made no move to visit anyone else. He seemed content to stand by her and polish off his burger. She soaked up his nearness. Their respective canoe positions kept them much too far apart to her way of thinking.

Jesse walked over. "Tell me about these cuts. They're next, right?"

Silas spoke up. "The river creates alternative paths around logjams. Similar to a maze, most paths don't go anywhere. Easy to get lost. Lose a lot of time."

"Lost?" Paige had joined them, her almond-shaped eyes round with trepidation. "Not really lost-lost."

"Swampy. Hard to navigate. Monsters." Silas uttered the last word with a deadpan expression.

Nat spooned the creamy green flesh of an avocado. She looked at the bite, deciding if it was worth the effort. Reluctantly, she scooped the bite into her mouth, talking around it. Her manners had faded along with her physical strength. "We got this, Paige. No worries."

Her friend didn't look the least bit convinced. Jesse rested a hand on her slim shoulder. "Each boat has a GPS tracker."

"Nat's right. We got this." Silas shot her a brief look full of something Nat couldn't decipher.

Monsters? Surely, he jested. All those weird stories they'd heard were pure embellishment. Nothing but outlandish fishing yarns.

Surely.

SILAS STOOD WITH NAT, waist-deep in the water, as they polished off their drinks. Anything to stay cool. He'd never underestimate the sun's power again. It completely zapped his drive.

Nat had tossed her empty drink bottle to Jesse. She now lay across the boat, her stomach resting on the seat, arms and legs hanging over the sides. Kid posture, except for nothing else about her appearance was childlike. Silas's gut flooded with warmth, thankful when she folded into the canoe.

"Our home away from home. C'mon, Sy. Let's fly this boat down the river." She attempted a peppy attitude, save for her droopy posture. They were both worn to a frazzle.

Silas gripped a fallen tree trunk to hoist his body into the canoe. He raised his hands in a mock high five. "We got this?"

Nat air-slapped his hands. "We got this!" Her palms were as red and blistered as his. Silas pushed the boat off. Nat started paddling.

"Wrong direction."

"Other way, sweetheart." Silas and Jesse called out together.

Nat swung her blade over to paddle the opposite way, shooting a grin at Silas.

Silas shook his head and kept paddling. Jesse stood on the bank, his fierce expression communicating a clear, simple message.

Leave my sister alone.

Resentment smoldered into hot coals inside Silas's chest. The man had to know throwing them together would push their relationship either way.

"Ignore my big brother." Nat broke into Silas's aggravation. "Jesse tries to intimidate any guy who gets within ten feet of me." She looked smug. "He needs to remember us doing this together was his brainchild. We can't help the circumstances."

Silas's bad feelings ebbed a tad. Nat had a pretty good handle on her protective older brother.

Diamonds of sunlight sparkled across the water. Bone-weary as they both were, Nat's paddle flowed as part of her body. Perfectly in sync. Would their paddling harmony extend beyond friendship? He'd grown to care about her. Silas shut down the thought before it sprouted a root. Elvis proved better at relationships than him.

Several miles down the river, Nat turned. "I need the question game to keep me awake."

Silas agreed. They had sung a few rounds. Nat had verbalized another long, loud prayer. He'd listened, enjoying her open, honest way of communicating with God. Well, barring the parts that made little sense. He frowned. Due to the prolonged lack of sleep and harsh conditions, Nat's sharp mind had softened around the edges.

"Ask me anything, sweet girl."

"Why do you call me a girl? I haven't been a girl for years." The plaintive way she said "girl" stirred his adrenaline.

"You're all woman, Nat. Girl is just a different way of saying it."

"You think I'm a woman?" She'd stopped paddling to run a hand through the water.

"Totally woman. No hands in the water. Keep paddling."

"Why? The water feels cool."

"Water moccasins in this area."

She snatched her hand out, then her brow wrinkled. Silas's heart sank. She held the paddle with no recognition as to its function.

Lord, help us both. "Paddle, Nat. Put the blade in the water."

A scowl marred her sunburnt cheeks. "I know what to do, silly."

They paddled in silence for a few minutes. Silas prayed furiously for the woman in the boat with him.

"Have you ever endured rejection, Silas?"

Silas snorted. Only from birth on. He answered carefully, uncertain if Nat was still in la-la land or if the question was legitimate. "Course I have. Haven't you?"

"Only in the sense that I don't measure up, though I'm starting to believe it's mostly self-imposed. Mom and Jesse have always loved me. Now, I realize Dad loved me, only he stunk at showing it. But Jesus loves me all the time, no matter what." She automatically increased her stroke rate to match his faster one.

Leave it to Nat to parse an unwieldy spiritual concept most folks wouldn't attempt to wrap their brains around. Was the gut-deep rejection he'd felt all of his life a product of his perceptions rather than reality? Gramps always said Silas's mom loved him as much as she was capable. No getting around her choices, but they were her choices, not because he wasn't worthy of love. The truth pebbled into his weary heart, bringing a kaleidoscope of color and light. And Nat.

He tuned back to Nat's semi-rambles. "So what I'm getting at is ... now that Christ lives in me, I have access to a whole new way of thinking. His way. I'm not bound by my old habits because I can embrace the way He does things." An emotional punch slammed into him as he observed the joy on her face. The slivers of color and light in his heart avalanched into a glorious understanding.

Following Christ wasn't another cause for worry. It was something to celebrate. Every. Single. Day. He had the freedom to carve out a new future instead of listening to the inner cynic who second-guessed and criticized every move.

CHAPTER TWENTY

Somewhere during the endless day, they'd switched positions, paddling until dusk blotted out the sun's last rays. Spanish moss hung from skeletal trees in the river. Mist rose off the water, lending to the eerie effect. Nat donned her life preserver. Despite the sticky air, goosebumps rose all over her body. She fought against the prickly sensation. Pesky mosquitoes hummed around her head as she slathered on repellant.

Her legs were cramping. Her stomach resembled a dishwasher—lots of cycling and swishing. The sun going down had become a source of dread. Odd. They'd already paddled through two nights. Surely, they could manage one more.

"You okay?" If she got her mind off herself …

"Yep." A lull ensued as they paddled. "You?"

His brief answer wasn't near enough. "Talk to me. It's getting weird up here."

"What do you want me to say, sweetheart?"

"Anything. Tell me about Gramps and Elvis."

A chuckle broke the moonlit night. "I told you Gramps raised me. Taught me how to fish. Kept me in school. After the Army stint, he watched out for me—encouraged me to do the higher learning thing. Not sure where I'd be if it weren't for him."

"When did y'all get Elvis?" Talking helped. Keeping her mind off the pain allowed her to match Silas's stroke rate.

"During my deployment, the dog we'd had for years died, so Gramps made the rounds at the shelters until he found Elvis. Gramps said they bonded right away. It's easy to tell"—a teasing note entered his voice— "Elvis thinks the world is his fan club. At the end of the day, though, he's all about Gramps. The letters he wrote at the time were full of his puppy antics.

"Those letters kept me sane. Gramps shared normal day-to-day stuff. It helped me to believe a decent life wasn't out of reach. Once I came home, I moved into a unit of his little apartment complex."

"Having family close by is good."

"For his sake and mine. He's cagey about his age, but he's got to be pushing eighty. Despite his grumping about Elvis, that dog keeps him going."

Nat blinked. She rubbed her eyes. A large rectangular building stood in the middle of the river. They were paddling right into it.

"Sy, do you see something up ahead?"

He peered past her. "What do you see?"

"A garage ... or a house. Is there a bend in the river? It keeps getting bigger."

"We'll get closer, then see what it is."

His steadiness reassured her. Until she realized he didn't see it. How could he not? It was ... enormous. White with funny doors. Lights glowed from within.

They paddled. And paddled. And paddled. Then the house disappeared.

"Where are we, Silas?" Nat shivered again.

"Hallucination Alley."

"WELL, THAT EXPLAINS A LOT." Her noise of disgust reached him. "My estimation is we're about halfway through the cuts. What do you think?"

Silas hoped so. The map he'd drawn on the inside of the boat wasn't helping. What he'd been so sure of on paper—or on the carbon fiber of the boat—didn't translate to current river conditions. It had a mind of its own, snaking in all directions until nothing looked familiar.

He'd lost the path.

"Silas."

"Give me a sec, Nat. Getting my bearings straight."

"Silas." Her paddle stopped.

He shifted impatiently on the seat cushion. "I'm figuring out—" The rest of it died as he looked to where she pointed.

Several sets of eyes glowed in the dark. Watching them. Bile rose in his throat. His paddle slowed.

"Please tell me you see them too," Nat rasped.

He exhaled softly. "Alligators. Other than menacing to look at, they've never bothered the paddlers."

"I'd rather not be the first." Apprehension filled her voice.

"We're good, unless we do something stupid."

"Got it. Don't be stupid."

Silas concurred. He mashed sore feet on the pedals to get the boat moving again. Something snapped. The pedals flapped uselessly, making no headway.

"Start praying, Nat."

She turned, her eyes round with fear. "Dare I ask why?"

"Steady, Nat."

"What happened?"

"The rudder cable broke."

"What are we going to do? We can't just stay on the river." Her last word ended in a high-pitched wail.

"We're going to fix it."

She took a shuddery breath. Then another. He inhaled a deep breath of his own. *Work the problem, soldier.*

Later, he couldn't explain or remember how he fixed the broken cable. Nat pried a strip of metal from the boat gunnel, and he fashioned a messy knot of sorts. It shortened the cable, making the pedals jerk. They were so wretchedly uncomfortable, one more ingredient into the mix had ceased to matter.

His heart thrashed, fully awakened, when Nat called him her hero. He'd do it again, even the alligators, to hear her say it again. Or not. The incessant darkness was yanking him down to a place he refused to let her go.

"Talk, Nat. Fire those questions at me." Anything to stay on track. Gramps talked about how mental acuity faded around the sixty-hour mark. That happened several hours ago. Drat this race, anyway. They were supposed to be ahead of the pack, not piddling around trying to find their way.

"Ever had a serious relationship?" Nat's cheery tone sounded too bright for the question.

His chest tightened. For the last three days, they'd covered their childhoods and all sorts of miscellaneous information. Their past relationships were bound to come up, though his mind balked at the gritty topic.

Silas took a deep breath, swiping the water with his blade. "A divorce several years ago." He'd forgotten the exact date, but not the grief. Or the emptiness.

In the dark, he sensed rather than saw her back stiffen. "I'm sorry. No way to reconcile?"

He pondered the question. Pastor Mike had helped him through the guilt that had plagued him for years. He hadn't wanted reconciliation. She'd moved on too. Finally, he said, "Neither of us wanted it."

They paddled in silence. Their boat glided snake-like through the water.

"How long did you date Colin?" Silas had instantly pegged the guy as all wrong for her.

She scowled, then her shoulders heaved. "Not long. From the start, I knew it wouldn't be long term—he had the opposite opinion. We fought all the time. He said he wanted to reconcile, but he didn't mean it. Not in a way I could live with. The hardest part has been forgiving myself for being so stupid."

Oh, Silas could relate. "You've been listening to Pastor Mike."

"He says it often enough. I've got another question."

"Fire away." It astonished him how easily they talked. He rarely spoke beyond absolute necessity.

"Do you have siblings?"

"A brother."

"Younger or older?"

"Younger." Silas hesitated. "He's special needs."

Nat didn't seem put off. "How so?"

"He's autistic."

Nat's silence encouraged him to keep going. "He was atypical even as a toddler, though it took a while to get a correct diagnosis."

"Bet that was hard for your mom."

Silas made a noise between a snort and a sigh. He stabbed the water with his oar. "Mom wasn't all that stable to begin with. Once she realized Petey wouldn't get over his condition, she basically washed her hands of both of us. Dropped us off with Gramps one weekend and never returned."

"Oh." She stroked, quietly digesting his revelation. "So Gramps raised you?"

"Yeah. We'd have been in foster care if not for Gramps."

"So where's Petey now?"

"When I went in the military, Gramps had to relocate him to a home for special needs adults. Not our favorite choice, yet it's better this way. Petey is strong physically. If he doesn't want to do something, he's more than Gramps can handle. I'm not around enough to be a real help."

"How often do you get to see him?"

"I get a visit in most weeks. Sometimes, we take him with us for an outing, but he's acclimated to the home. He gets antsy if he's away too long."

Nat moved the paddle as if an extension of her arm. "Once we're done with this blasted race, I want to meet him."

"Why?" Silas's burned-out brain formulated the single-word question. The deeper part of him nagged for more.

"Now that you've told me about Petey, it's easy to understand how you connect with unique clients. The way you bonded with Emily. The root of your gentleness with a special-needs toddler is Petey."

Silas paddled. What Nat said made sense. He'd spent years coaxing Petey on basic life skills. It filled him with such purpose, nothing else compared. So, yeah, helping people learn or relearn how to use their limbs came naturally. A new appreciation for the power of love washed through the encroaching darkness.

They paddled on, doing their dead-level best to stay on the river. Way too easy to veer into a cut leading nowhere. Swampy. Misty. Steam spiraling up from the water created an ethereal effect. The bayous had nothing on this stretch of watery labyrinth.

Silas recognized a familiar tree stump. Aww, nuts. They were going in circles. Suddenly, Nat shrieked, thrashing her paddle at the air. Silas worked to balance the boat. "Quit. Nat, stop," he yelled. The screaming subsided, but Nat kept burrowing into the canoe.

"What is it? Are you hurt?" Silas's pulse jumped all over the place.

Nat slung an arm behind her, pointing at something. She cried, "Swamp Thing. Back that way!"

Silas looked, then yelled back, "It's not there."

Except Nat thought differently. She paddled frantically. Silas paddled too, except they weren't in sync. She kept rowing toward the bank where the alligators crouched watchfully.

For heaven's sake, didn't she see them? "No, Nat. The other way!"

As he steered the canoe the other way, her strokes became less panicked. A wide cut off appeared ahead. "It's the way out." Nat shouted.

"It's *not* the way out."

"It is! I see another canoe."

"Doesn't mean anything."

Nat mumbled something incoherent. Silas didn't answer. His mental lapses were hindering rational perception. He couldn't find the way. Where was God? Why didn't He help them?

The thing he feared most had happened. They were lost. Any lucid thought crumbled as numbness wrapped him in despair. They wouldn't finish the race. Their futures were gone.

He croaked, "I'm sorry." His head dropped. Raising it again proved too much trouble. His world spun into ash.

CHAPTER TWENTY-ONE

"Silas. Silas, wake up." Nat poked him with her blade. They'd both fallen asleep. Who knew how far they'd drifted? Or where? The Spanish moss hanging from the trees contributed to the spooky atmosphere. Silas stayed huddled over, head almost in his lap. Dead to the world. "Wake up, bud."

He pushed at her oar, then looked back. The dim whites of his eyes revealed his dismal state. Rubbing a hand over his face, he squinted at her. "Nat." A question lingered around the syllable. "Where are we?"

"Somewhere on Alligator Lake, I think."

He nodded. "The cuts. We're lost?"

"Yes." Pleased that he sounded reasonably lucid, Nat wished him a speedy return to sanity. Especially since hers blinked in and out.

"Ahoy, weary travelers!" Warily, Nat shaded her eyes against the bright bow light coming toward them. Why hadn't she seen it before now? The calm swish of a paddle gliding through the water came near. Past the light, she spied a man in a boat.

"Hi, uh, sir." Normally, she didn't address men as "sir." They didn't seem to appreciate it coming from her, yet it had slipped out with no conscious thought. "Do you know where we are?" Nat asked. Hopefully, the guy was a decent human being, not given to murdering people. He didn't look like a killer, not that she'd met one before. Just a regular guy, no distinguishing characteristics—except for the red knit cap— too warm for summer in south Texas.

"Yes. You looking for the way out?"

"We've been paddling in circles, so yes. We'd be grateful for directions." Relief filled Nat at Silas's gravelly response. Polite. Minus the reluctance usually accompanying his speech.

A brilliant smile tipped the stranger's mouth. "I'll show you the way. Follow me."

He set the perfect pace. As they adapted their stroke rate to his, Nat intercepted Silas's incredulous gaze. His eyes asked, *Are you experiencing this too?* Oddly enough, her side no longer ached. The man called out directions and pointed out landmarks they'd both overlooked. It all appeared perfectly plain. The exhaustion sloughed off, replaced by an unusual refreshing.

"Are you enjoying the race?" their guide asked. Nat didn't remember saying anything about the race. Enjoying it? Getting shot at hardly qualified, yet this stranger seemed serious.

As she searched for a diplomatic answer, Silas said, "It's been challenging joing."

"More challenging than enjoyable," Nat admitted with a nod.

"Mm. If you'll focus on the joys of doing it together, it won't be so hard." Earnestness layered the stranger's words like thick frosting.

She exchanged another look with Silas. *Who was this guy?*

Nat made to follow in his wake, but his boat had disappeared.

Silas's blade gouged the water in frustration. "Where did he go?"

Nat peered into the fog. "He's gone." Gentle sounds of night stirred. She perceived new strength for the rest of their journey. "Are you thinking what I'm thinking?"

Silas's eyes glowed. "Let's save the million-dollar question for later. Right now, I'd rather leave the alligators behind."

INVIGORATED, Silas didn't know whether to credit the untimed nap or the encounter with the stranger. Eerie how he appeared just when they were on the verge of giving up. Certainty zinged into his spirit. Meeting the stranger had been no coincidence.

Oh, man. He picked up their stroke rate, willing Nat to catch up. Since Mr. Red Cap had kindly pointed out landmarks, Silas knew exactly where they were. They'd done practice runs through this section twice but never at night.

How did the guy say it? Focus on doing it together ... for enjoyment? What did that mean, aside from the normal cooperate-with-your-partner advice? Throughout the course of the race, Nat frustrated him. Irked him. Aggravated him.

And he'd fallen in love with her.

At the start, though, her motor scooter injuries had almost annoyed him, consumed as he was about the race outcome. Disgust washed over him in a wave.

The gunshots only proved it again. Never mind the danger. Annoyance had been his chief emotion about her little pink flag. Part of him received the barest scrap of satisfaction when the sniper demolished it. Why shouldn't she enjoy her girlie tribute to the race? If a simple flag made her happy, why did he have to throw a wet blanket on it? Realization slapped him. He had contributed to her "trying too hard" mentality. Yeah, his attraction to her helped to mellow a few reactions, yet she deserved so much more.

He'd been a jerk.

Silas wanted to bare his soul to God with Nat's transparency. Minus the yelling. Still paddling, eyes on the river, he muttered under his breath. "Lord, I've messed up, especially with my attitude about Nat. I'm sorry. Thanks for revealing it to me. Thanks for sending the stranger. Thanks for letting me do this with her." The stark truth presented itself. "You know I'm crazy about her. I didn't see the gift she is. I get there's nothing I can do to deserve her ... but I promise to treat her better."

"Silas," Nat called. He looked where she had pointed. He whiffed salty air. Were they really this close to the Saltwater Barrier dam? His stomach churned as they paddled closer. A massive logjam blocked the entire river. He instinctively knew there would be no Red Sea moment when God parted the waters this time.

Since their encounter with the stranger, he'd gained a buoyancy, a confidence that had eluded him the entire race. His body, however, argued mightily as he climbed out of the canoe. Nat followed, taking hold of the towline outside the bow. The woman had no quit bone.

Two separate multi-man teams had holed up on the left bank. As Silas listened to their conversation, it became clear they didn't know how to portage around the next two obstacles—the enormous logjam and the submerged dam. Another tandem team had gone into the man-made canal. No one had heard from them since.

He couldn't explain how, but he knew the way through. His gaze met Nat's. He was most sorry for the price it would extract from her. He whistled loudly, and all conversation ceased. The other teams looked at them expectantly. "Whoever wants to follow, I can get us past the logjam," Silas said.

Moving to her, he lowered his voice. "Long portage ahead. I'll do the heavy lifting."

Her hand found his. "We can do this."

He leaned so close, the heat coming off her sunburned cheeks warmed him. "I wish you didn't have to."

"Thank you." For the barest moment, her eyes telegraphed pain. Her throat moved as she swallowed. The tiniest twitch of her lips betrayed ... hope? For them? He wanted it too.

Nat made her way back to the canoe. She took hold of the towline, resolve etched in each slow movement. They headed to the right, picking their way through the rocks on the side of the dam. Silas took a deep breath. The two-mile portage would zap what little energy they had left. He bowed his head. "Lord, we're countin' on You for the impossible."

"CALHOUN RETREAT AHEAD. THE LAST CHECKPOINT," he called out, breathless. Fog blanketed the river, competing with the pre-dawn light. Silas squinted to see beyond the boat ramp to the newly built platform. They glided across the water to the wooden posts on the left bank.

Silas tied off the boat, then climbed out to help Nat. "Find a grassy patch and rest. I'll bring food."

Her lack of argument spoke volumes about her physical state. Silas watched with concern as she gingerly took a few steps to a green area. Her descent turned into an uncontrolled plop. More worrisome was her unfocused gaze. Hopefully, this brief stop would set her to rights. Despite the early hour, people milled about, eating and drinking. Others napped on the hard ground.

A familiar bark floated on the air, and Elvis twined around Silas. The canine wriggled all over with happiness. He grabbed a fistful of the dog's fur as Gramps put a carton of warm spaghetti in his hand. Before he took a bite, he glanced back at Nat. Mike had already reached her with a protein shake.

The cozy campground enticed him to stay. "Where's Lacy?"

Gramps lifted his shoulders with a grunt. "Still gettin' her beauty sleep?"

Silas's stomach rumbled. After a tentative first bite, he couldn't fork it in his mouth fast enough. Gramps spoke. "One more stretch to go, bud. How're you and your sweet little gal doing?"

He ignored the reference to Nat being his. "We're good. The portage around the logjam was hellacious." Gramps's nod communicated far more than mere acknowledgment. He understood what Silas hadn't said as well. Silas grabbed a Gatorade, then searched for Nat again. She was nibbling on something bright orange. Sweet potato? It would fit with her theories on nutrition. Silas had only ever eaten sweet potato at Thanksgiving—doctored with brown sugar and marshmallows. He'd finagle a bite of hers since she rarely finished any food.

"You listenin' to me, boy?"

Silas tuned back to Gramps. The older man looked pale. His skin resembled the inside of a banana peel. "Sorry. Say it again —I need every pearl of wisdom you've got." Silas found himself so stinking grateful for the man standing before him, it took all he had not to enclose him in a bear hug.

Gramps didn't hesitate. "You need to dump what you don't need from the boat. It's gonna be a choppy ride across the bay.

The wind is up. Keep your wits. You hit the wall of mental compromise hours ago."

Yeah, his thoughts had squished around with no substance for some time. He said, "We've come this far. I'll see you at the finish line."

"You will. Proud of you, son. Gone too far to quit now. Doesn't make no difference if you walk the boat in or paddle. There's still a badge waiting for you. You've earned it either way."

Everything in him wanted to paddle across the finish line in grand style. However, he had far more pressing matters at the moment. His urge for a bite of sweet potato had grown to epic proportions. From a lady far too good for him.

CHAPTER TWENTY-TWO

Nat stared uncomprehendingly. Why was the boat full of water? "What happened?"

Silas had stilled next to her. "Let's dump it out, get it on the bank." His words rang low and furious.

Together, they stood in the river. They tipped the canoe, so the water drained, then hefted it upside down onto a tangle of tree roots. Nat's exhaustion fled in the face of this new threat. Was the boat damaged beyond repair? What if they couldn't finish the race?

With short, clipped movements betraying his anger, Silas ran his hands along one side, obviously searching for a leak. He rubbed his fingers into three different places as he waded next to the boat. His scowl grew deeper each time. Then he moved to the other side and gave it a cursory swipe.

Gazing at the river with a clenched jaw, he reached for her hand. "We have to talk."

"Tell me." She shook her head at the sandwich Mike offered her.

"Tell both of us." Mike made no move to go.

Silas expelled a hard breath. "Someone sabotaged our boat."

Initially, the news shocked Nat into silence, then she found her voice. "Are you sure?" She slung an arm around the campground. "There are scads of people around."

Silas gave a brief jerk of his head. "Three holes made by a knife."

Mike, who'd been quiet up to this point, spoke. "Easy enough to do, foggy as it is. The guy brushed against the boat and paddled off with no one the wiser. Are you going to inform the racing official?"

"Yeah, for all the good it'll do." Silas turned his head. He spit into a patch of weeds, something Nat recognized as a sign of agitation. "It was deliberate." His eyes found hers. "Your ex has stepped up his game. Whoever he hired might still be here, waiting to see what we do."

"But—"

Shaking his head, he squeezed her hand. "First the gunshots. Now this."

Mike's brows climbed at the mention of gunshots. Favoring Silas with a hard look, he said, "First I've heard about gunshots." He gestured to the boat. "Sure sounds as if somebody doesn't want you to finish."

Nat froze. "What?"

"These *criminal acts* remain excellent reasons to choose *safety* over the race. Where's your thinking on this?"

"Silas left the decision to stay in the race up to me," Nat objected. "*I* insisted we continue."

"The shooter had accomplished what he came to do. We weren't the target." Silas had slid behind her and placed his hands on her shoulders in a protective stance.

Even as Nat reveled in his touch, her mind roiled with confusion. "Why would Colin bother to mess up our race? It seems so … beneath him.”

Silas spoke next to her ear. “Is he the jealous type?”

She considered the question, then shrugged. “He despised Jesse.”

“Anyone else?”

Nat slowly shook her head. “No other guy in the picture for him to be jealous of.”

“There is now,” Mike inserted. Nat felt rather than saw Silas’s scowl. The blade of grass she fingered crumpled into a ball as the words registered.

“If you think he’s jealous of Silas, that’s crazy. We’re only here to keep our futures at Peeps.”

“You think that’s what everyone else sees?” Mike sounded unconvinced. He stared directly at Silas’s hands, still resting on her shoulders. “Y’all have spent a lot of time together. Silas’s theory is valid. Jealousy is akin to covetousness. If a person dwells on any negative emotion enough, it’s liable to get out of hand. Rational thought goes out the window. Illogical decisions become the norm.”

“No, Colin’s MO is control. He hates stupidity. I highly doubt he’d be jealous of us. He’s more the type to cut his losses and move on.” Even as she said the words, something Colin said once vied for attention. *I want you all for myself.*

Silas gave her shoulders one last squeeze. “I need to tell the official, then patch the boat.” He peered around. The sun had been steadily burning through the fog, clearing away the haze. “It will need time to dry.” He came around to gaze at her, a mix of tenderness and torture in his eyes. “Rest. Sleep if you can. Gramps and Elvis will keep you company.”

His quick whistle brought Elvis, with Gramps following. Silas pointed at her. The dog burrowed next to her legs with a zest Nat envied. Her insides cartwheeled sloppily as she petted him. Gramps eased down beside her. Despite her defense of their motives, Mike had already seen what she hadn't admitted until now. Was this what it felt like to love someone? A soft glow warmed her. Silas tramped off to find the race official, cowboy hat trailing down his back, Mike on his heels.

Hurry back, love.

"YOU'RE NOT SERIOUSLY THINKING of continuing the race, are you?" Mike leaned down next to where Silas kneeled at the boat.

He applied a patch to the first slit in the canoe, then covered it sparingly with the rest of the adhesive. "It's up to Nat. As scary as it sounds, we haven't been in danger."

"What about the gunshots?"

"I told you, the shooter only wanted to frighten us."

"What if his shooting wasn't as good as yours? What if he missed? Sounds to me the window of opportunity stayed sketchy." Mike's affable manner had vanished.

Silas tamped his thumb on the tape, then scooted to the next slit. "Okay. I'll concede gunfire is nothing to play around with. But nothing else happened until now. Think about it. The boat got damaged. We're fine." He pressed against the tape edges with his fingertips.

Mike shook his head. "No shame in extenuating circumstances making you decide to stop."

"The deal is we finish the race. Our futures are on the line." Silas kept his face averted. If he looked at Mike, he'd rile up faster than a territorial dog.

"You've told me how it came about. Surely, Mr. Spence will understand. Getting shot at is enough for any rational person. Now someone sabotaged your boat. Plenty of reason not to put yourselves in more danger."

"It is." Silas echoed a perfunctory agreement, though he wasn't convinced Mr. Spence and Jesse's solution to their prank had been reasonable in the first place. "Here's what I know. Any attempt to put Nat in bubble wrap will backfire. My gut tells me there's more to this than she wants to believe, but it's still her call."

"I hope you're planning to pursue a relationship with her."

The abrupt change of topic whirled Silas into overdrive. "She doesn't want a relationship with me."

"Who says?" Mike demanded.

"You heard her. She's only doing this with me because she has to." A bitter note crept into the words. He pried a corner of the tape loose, then pushed it down again.

"Yeah, I heard. It sounded more like denial to me. All of her actions say otherwise. Silas, what's keeping you closed off? You two are magnets—literally pulling toward each other—it's as obvious as day following night."

"She doesn't know me."

"Nat's spent three days and nights in a boat with you. She knows you better than you know yourself. Trust me, she's interested."

Silas's dry eyes bulged. "Dude, you know my sorry history. I'm no good at relationships, especially with women."

"I know you recommitted your life to Christ. He makes all things new. If you submit your relationship to Him, He'll keep you in check."

"I'll mess it up."

"You both will. It's how you learn to communicate. You get it wrong, talk it out, then stumble along until the next time."

"You make it sound easy."

Mike shook his head and flashed him a wicked grin. "Oh, it's not easy. But a good marriage far outweighs the trouble."

The feelings Silas had previously tamped down roared with

desire, but he didn't trust them. He couldn't make any serious decision in his dicey mental state. One coherent thread deep inside insisted it was okay to be in love with Nat. Maybe she'd listen if he could find the courage to bare his heart.

First, however, they had to finish the race.

CHAPTER TWENTY-THREE

Without a word, Nat hiked one leg, then the other, into the dry, patched canoe. Rays of sun beat down on the water, causing a sparkler effect.

"Are you sure, Nat? We still have to get across the bay. The finish might be horrendous." Silas had eased into the boat on the stern end. Instead of grabbing a paddle, he looked at her, waiting.

"Yes. I prayed about it. All I know is this—if I succumb to the way I feel, I'll always regret it. I'm guessing it's no different for you." A flicker of relief crossed his face before it went back to unreadable. Fuzziness crowded her peripheral vision. Yet they'd come too far now. She picked up her paddle, digging into the glistening river with resolve. Gramps hollered encouragement as they paddled downstream.

No such thing as an easy finish to the Texas Water Safari. The bay presented a unique set of obstacles. The wind blew her cowboy hat from her head as if to emphasize the hardships.

"Let's do fast-slow."

Her mind stayed too frazzled for any kind of verbal

motivation, so she dipped her blade, keeping pace with his fast strokes. "One, two, three ..." he counted off in a lively manner, his paddle churning up the clear water. Did the guy have no stop button?

Once he wound down, Nat picked up the cadence at a less hectic pace. "One slow, two slow, three slow ..." She drew out the words. Her hands stilled on the paddle. More alligators. They slithered into the river, their bodies resembling logs floating on the water. "Your turn, Silas!" The more space between them and the loathsome creatures, the happier she'd be.

The cloudiness in her brain didn't dissipate as she'd hoped. Instead, it increased. She mimicked Silas's moves on automatic pilot. Good thing they'd decided ahead of time which way they'd go. They steered into San Antonio Bay, then paddled along the shoreline.

The wind threatened to rip the sunglasses from her face. Silas shouted something. She cupped a hand to her ear to show her lack of hearing.

He shook his head, then pulled his paddle out of the water. Sighing, she placed her paddle across the boat. Ferocious gusts blew them back the way they came. Silas hopped out of the boat near a point of land and towed them to it.

"What?" The tiny rational part of her understood the belligerent tone wasn't helping. Seriously, why couldn't they just get this race over with?

"The wind is treacherous."

"But we're so close."

"The boat will flip. It might break. We have to sit it out and hope the wind dies enough to try it again."

She stared at him. His hat had fallen down his back. The wind whipped his shaggy hair into a tousled mess. His eyes willed her to believe him.

Another sigh escaped. "This is a nightmare."

"The pain is talking. Let's find a place to chill." He plodded through the tall grass. Putting his sunglasses back on, he peered around.

Shells crunched under Nat's water shoes as she followed him.

A short distance in, an abandoned fishing camp emerged. A rotting, briny smell rose, wrinkling her nose. An old tarp stretched between three rickety poles. Charcoal remains nestled in the sand. An assortment of cans littered the area. A rusty trash barrel stood several feet away. Nat shivered. The wind prickled her skin.

Silas moved to her. "Let's sit together. You need to stay warm."

Nat sat on a log next to the ancient campfire. She had no reserves left. He sat so close, she inhaled his river scent.

"Why are we here?" If only she could remember things better …

"To build a house."

His explanation made no sense. "That's not why we're here. Why would we build a house?"

He leaned closer, nestling her under his arm. "To live in, silly. Why else?"

She scratched a mosquito bite on her hand. "It needs a—" The word floated up sluggishly from the foggy depths of her compromised gray matter. "—roof. To keep the mosquitoes out."

Silas shot her a grin. "Of course. A house with no roof won't help with mosquitoes." He paused. "Why are we doing this?"

"Doing what? We're just sitting here."

His thick brow knitted. "The canoe."

It sounded familiar. Still, Nat couldn't put her finger on it.

She didn't want to leave the warmth Silas provided. "I'm not ready to get in a boat."

"Me neither." Silas stretched his legs out in front of him.

Nat couldn't take her eyes off his feet. "Where are your shoes?"

He gazed at his feet as if seeing them for the first time. "I don't have any."

"Yes, you do. A pair of—" A giggle slipped out when the word wouldn't come.

Silas grinned again. He had the best smile. "As I said. No shoes." He peered at the sky. "We better build our house before it rains. With a fireplace." He took her hand and gently pulled. "Up-sa daisy."

"Up-sa daisy," Nat echoed.

THE SLIGHT LUCIDITY Silas experienced back at the last checkpoint had poofed. Nothing Nat said made a lick of sense either, except she was beautiful with the cowboy hat hanging down her back, and that ponytail whipping every which way. Why they were here eluded him. A glimpse would come, then it'd be gone before he could focus. He had to take care of Nat, though. He'd promised.

He dropped the piece of metal he'd picked up and went to help her. What a keeper. She'd gathered sticks in pioneer woman style. "I think you need to sit by me again." He reached for a stick, still trying to remember. It was important.

She pushed his hand away. "It's for the fire."

"We don't have a fire, Nat." He sat down, patting the place beside him. "Sit."

She shrugged, dropping the sticks to join him. "You keep

me warm." She mumbled something under her breath. It made no sense either.

Silas draped an arm around her. A stinky trash barrel had nothing on him. But her? She only grew prettier. Except for the laceration on her side. She'd winced when he squeezed her waist.

"It hurts a lot?"

She lay her head on his shoulder. "Yes."

Silas stroked her hair. As soft as he'd imagined. "Let me get your mind off the pain."

She straightened. Looked him full in the face, a slightly quizzical expression knitting her brows. "No more ointment."

The pebbly skin on her lips drew him closer. Her breath warmed his cheeks. "Not what I had in mind."

"Oh." Her eyes dropped to his lips.

He ran a thumb down her cheek. A distant alarm clanged in his mind. He pulled back. A gnat's hair. A tiny smile rife with impishness darted through Nat's tawny eyes. She gripped his shirt in her fists, drawing him closer. "Make the pain go away, cowboy."

His lips covered hers, demanding her attention. She kissed him back freely, echoing his insistence on the here and now. His arms tightened around her shoulders as the kiss deepened.

"Hey, lovebirds! Are y'all part of the canoe race?" A man with a fishing pole hollered at them.

Reluctantly, he pulled back, still holding her. "Canoe race?"

"Yeah. The Texas Water Safari. I saw your boat." He came closer, face grizzled from years in the sun.

Silas searched for an answer. His head swam with fragmented questions.

With a gasp, Nat stirred in his arms. "Sy! The canoe race. We have to finish."

Desire warred as his mind struggled to grasp what they were saying. "We're building a house."

"No, babe." She wiggled out of his arms. Well, shucks. He needed more snuggle time. "Has the wind died down?" She looked at the fisherman, then back at him.

He stared into her warm, tea-colored eyes. They implored him to do—what?

"Has the wind died down?" She repeated, not so patiently.

An amused expression peeked through the fisherman's white, whiskery cheeks. "Better than earlier, but it's still a hard go."

"C'mon, Sy." She grabbed his hand. "We have to try. We've come too far to quit."

Quit? He couldn't quit. He had to see this done. *See what done?* An inner voice mocked him. Frantically, he searched for answers. The words formed before awareness kicked in. "Help me, Lord."

Instantly, his brain fog cleared as if someone pulled the stopper jamming his ability to think. The canoe race! They had to finish.

Nat led him to the sandy bank. To their red boat with the nicknames Gramps had emblazoned on the side.

He gazed at his hand entwined with Nat's. The memory of their fiery kiss stole across his mind. Despite the interruption, it left him reeling.

Hang the race. He wanted to kiss Nat again.

CHAPTER TWENTY-FOUR

They snapped on the boat skirt to keep the sea spray out, then eased back into the choppy bay. Waves slapped against the sides as if warning them not to proceed. Nat stuck her oar in, willing it through the rough water. *Onward Christian soldier, marching off to war...*words from the old hymn welled up from a place inside she'd forgotten. Mom took her and Jesse to the little church a block away from their house years ago. A sweet, comforting place when her young mind couldn't process Dad's lengthy absences. The place where God was near.

As she battled to complete stroke after stroke in the distressed waters, a strong assurance swept over her. God had always been with her. He'd never left. She'd been the one to run away. Hurt. Mad. She'd blamed God for everything. Instead of digging in, she'd run from his help and pushed away all who loved her. Especially Jesse.

Water sprayed her face, making her backward glimpses of Silas unclear as he fought the waves with his strong paddling skills. Far superior to hers. Swiping water from her eyes, she knew. Tough as she pretended to be, she would not have made it this far on her own.

The waves threatened to tip the boat. She glanced at the water pooling on the boat bottom. No way the bilge pump would work effectively in these volatile conditions.

"We're taking on water," Silas yelled over the noisy waves. He dug in again. Plowing through mud made more sense. The wind danced a wicked two-step. With each forward stroke they managed, the wind flung them back twice as far.

They stroked on opposite sides to keep the boat balanced, except when a vicious wave attacked, she lost their rhythm. Two strokes on the wrong side tipped the boat into the unwieldy surf.

Nat flailed around underneath the water, caught in the small hole of the spray skirt. Silas ripped the skirt away so she could surface. She gulped breaths of salty air. Seawater trickled down her throat. She coughed to rid her lungs of it. She'd have to thank him for saving her from drowning later.

The water reached their waists, still high enough to make moving the boat a cumbersome task. She waded toward the half-submerged canoe as Silas yelled vile things at the wind.

"Help me get it upright," Silas shouted once he'd finished his diatribe.

They each grabbed an end. Another wave crashed over them, adding more water to the canoe. Any attempt to climb back in would be counterproductive. "We have to guide it in," Nat screamed to make herself heard over the roar of the waves.

She hung on to the bowline. The wind mimicked a rebellious horse, yanking the canoe in all directions. Nat refused to let go. After repeated attempts to angle the boat over the crashing waves, they established a scrabbly sort of jog and carried the boat to the finish line. Nat's legs wobbled. The muddy bottom of the bay sucked at her feet, making it hard to keep her balance. Silas wore a look of exhilaration as he dragged the canoe up the cement boat ramp.

"We did it, Sy!" She wanted to celebrate their win. A quiet meal, the two of them firmly ensconced in a stationary restaurant booth. No water. For the first time since they'd started the race, hunger slammed into her.

"That we did." Sy's voice floated back. After tying the boat off, he returned to her. Gripping her arm, he pulled her mired feet out of the muck. She latched onto him for support as she regained her footing. Nat stumbled out of the bay with heartfelt thanks.

Silas slid an arm around her to help her up the steps next to a boat ramp. She looked around the crescent finger of the bay shore, slightly deflated not to see anyone they knew. Trucks and trailers filled the parking lot. People grouped around picnicking tables on the far side. A race official stood by, recording their time. Not that they won anything. Despite all the obstacles, they had finished their first Texas Water Safari! Her heart threatened to burst with their accomplishment, though her side throbbed in pain.

Out of nowhere Lacy came striding toward them, her face twisted into a grimace. Great.

Shooting Nat a hateful look, Lacy threaded her arm through Silas's. Her head close to his, her other arm gestured wildly as she drew him aside.

As Nat followed, a man wearing an official lanyard appeared with a clipboard. He handed her two badges. "Congratulations, miss. You and your partner completed the Texas Water Safari."

Nat accepted the badges, wishing for Silas by her side. Once Lacy finished talking, he strode to his car, not looking back. Strange.

"Silas," Nat broke into a slow trot to catch up, but Lacy blocked her path.

"Mike took Silas's grandfather to the emergency room."

Something happened to Gramps? "I'm going with Silas."

Lacy caught her by the arm. "No, I told him I'd bring you later. I figured you'd want to clean up first. There's no way they'll let you see him, though, not being family."

Nat tugged, wanting her arm back. Silas would understand her less than optimal appearance. Lacy's grip tightened. "He said you'd be trouble."

Silas thought she'd be trouble? Why would he think that? Nat wrestled to free her arm. She wouldn't interfere with a doctor's instructions. Engrossed in trying to figure out what Silas meant, her attention drifted. Until Lacy pointed a pistol at her.

Nat stilled, staring at the silvery weapon, then at the woman holding it. Cold blue eyes bored into her. "Someone wants to see you."

"What are you talking about?" Granted, her mental processes were snailish, except none of this made sense. "Who wants to see me?" Frantically casting about for answers, she spied a car in the parking lot. Fear careened through her stomach. Colin.

Lacy made certain Nat saw the gun again. "Let's not keep him waiting."

WORRY for Gramps crowded Silas's mind. He'd hated his abrupt exit, except Lacy insisted it was urgent. He had to get to the hospital ASAP. Emptiness filled him. Already he missed Nat, as if she'd been physically torn from him.

His eyes narrowed. Lifting his foot off the accelerator, he

stared in the rearview mirror at the scene unfolding behind him. Lacy had Nat by the arm—something Nat would never put up with—as they headed to a car. A flash of silver—a weapon. Images clicked through his mind at light speed. Lacy's hostility toward Nat. Her scooter accident. Nat arguing with her boyfriend in the Peeps' parking lot beside a sleek vehicle. The identical car they headed toward.

A man climbed out of the car and took Nat's other arm. Silas's pulse galloped with the need to act. He eased into a vacant parking place at the far end of the lot, his mind groping for a plan. He climbed out of his car to rummage behind the seat. A red Jeep zoomed toward him. Silas waved his arms. Jesse slammed on the brakes as Silas put a finger to his lips.

Jesse jumped out of the Jeep. "Did y'all finish? Where's Nat?"

"Pretty sure the ex-boyfriend has her." He pulled out a rifle case hidden beneath other gear.

Jesse's lips twisted into a snarl. "Colin." His face blanched when he spied the rifle case, though his voice remained steady. "Got a better plan? You're gonna get arrested with that."

Silas stared at the rifle case, then wanted to slap his forehead. In his fuzzy state, he'd defaulted to combat skills. Of all the stupid ... A high-powered rifle wouldn't help. Not in close quarters.

Frantically readjusting his mindset from sniper to ... helping Nat, he said, "My phone's still in the canoe. Call nine-one-one ... Tavo ... or whoever. We need backup. There's only one exit, so they'll have to leave this way." He frowned, finding it hard to concentrate, much less solve Nat's desperate dilemma.

Jesse stabbed at the buttons on his phone. In a low, terse voice, he talked to someone on the other end. He listened, then lapsed into impatient Spanish, his face growing redder by the second. Finally, he clicked off with grim satisfaction. "Help is on the way."

"I've heard you're good with your hands. Is it true?" Silas didn't refer to carpentry skills. Jesse, being a vet, would understand. "If the rifle stays in the truck, hand-to-hand is our only option."

Jesse nodded, his face stony. "Got it."

Silas motioned for Jesse to follow. He'd been in tighter spots on more missions than he could count. This one threatened to devastate him. He savagely slung back the emotions crawling all over him, an entire army of biting ants. Colin might have the upper hand now, but Silas would regain it. The woman he loved was in danger. Nothing would keep him from Nat.

They ducked, weaving between the vehicles to get closer.

CHAPTER TWENTY-FIVE

Nat gritted her teeth. Her mind clogged with the certainty of defeat. All the self-defense moves in the world wouldn't help her now. The guy holding her resembled a train car. Lacy backed away, holding the gun with shaky hands.

Colin emerged from the backseat of the silver car. Months ago, he'd proudly told Nat the make and model of his latest vehicle. She'd found the info boring. Now she'd happily key the paint off his sweet ride.

"Get rid of the gun, Lace," he said, not looking at the other woman. For once, Nat had all his attention. His eyes roved over her. Heat filled her at his hungry look. *Not happening, bud.* She lifted her chin, determined not to let him affect her. How had she ever thought him attractive?

Lacy appeared dazed. She looked at the thug who had Nat's arm in a vise grip. He jerked his head toward the bay. Lacy gave him a quizzical look, then moved to where he nodded, her steps picking up speed.

Nat's tired brain stayed mum with ideas on how to free her hands.

"So why'd you disappear, Nat?" Colin's velvety voice held a hint of hurt. Even in her sorry state, Nat knew better than to believe his concerned-boyfriend façade.

"Tell your thug to let go of me. Then we'll talk."

Colin's eyes narrowed as he motioned to the guy holding her. "Let go. Stay close though. This one knows how to defend herself." His sarcastic tone conveyed the exact opposite. He stood, hands in his pockets. "You left without a word, Nat. And you lectured *me* about communication." His gaze mocked her. "I imagined all sorts of bad things happening to you." Colin raised condescension to an art.

"I bet you did." The flexed jaw, however, gave him away. He might sound calm, even reasonable, but his emotional fuse had always been notoriously short. Another reason she'd left. However, not responding ticked him off, so she'd bide her time.

One perfect brow arched as if he read her thoughts. "Frankly, I'm impressed. You persevered through the obstacles. Chalk one up for finishing your stupid canoe race. One last silly goal accomplished in your little world before you come live in mine."

Biding her time instantly grew old. "I'm not going anywhere with you."

"Oh, I beg to differ. You see, I suspect you know too much. Fortunately for you, my feelings are ... quite strong where you're concerned. In time, I believe you'll grow as fond of me as I am of you."

His smirk sent her over the edge. "You're delusional. It will never happen, you filthy piece of ... " Still, she couldn't say the word that thrust from the dregs of her former life.

Colin's eyes glittered dangerously. "Coarse language doesn't become you, *dear*. Is it part of your mission to convert me from—what did you call it?—my state as a sinner?" As her mouth dropped open, his lip raised in disdain. "You thought I wasn't listening, but that's not entirely accurate. I heard you quite well. The truth is, being a sinner has its advantages. It's a lot more, ah, *rewarding* than the do-gooder stuff you peddle." He ran a thumb over manicured nails. "I suppose hanging out with your canoe partner helped lower your standards. Generous of you to take pity on his ugly mug."

Silas? Ugly? How dare Colin insult the finest person she knew? Fresh adrenaline spiked through her veins. She ignored the don't-let-him-push-your-buttons warning telegraphing across her brain.

Stepping forward, she smacked Colin across the face. Surprised, he reeled backward, clutching at his cheek.

Colin's thug lunged toward her with a long, snaky arm. She scuttled out of his reach. To her astonishment, a man jumped in front of her. Lean, powerful arms shoved him away.

Jesse.

Where had he come from? When the guy came at him again, Jesse fisted a lethal blow to his face. The thug stopped to grab his nose. Jesse took the opportunity to get behind him and sling an arm around his neck. Applying pressure, he held on tight. Nat's jaw sagged as the guy's eyes rolled back. None too gently, Jesse helped his crumpling body to the ground.

A homing pigeon, she stepped toward her brother until a hand gripped her mouth from behind. Colin snatched her to his chest, his arm a steel vise around her middle. His jagged breathing blew hot bursts on her neck. He shouted at Jesse. "Stay away or I hurt her."

Lightheadedness flooded Nat. She stomped on his foot. Colin howled, turning the air blue with curses. He scuffled with her, squeezing her into submission.

Jesse held his hands up. "It's over, Colin. The cops are on their way. Using her for leverage will only rack up more charges."

"They have to catch me first." His punishing hold hindered her ability to breathe. If Jesse didn't do something—her eyes bulged.

Her vision blackened. Suddenly, the pressure on her mouth and waist relented. Colin doubled over, limp as a fish. Jesse pushed him back, then wrapped Nat in a hug as she stumbled away. She gasped for air as her eyes tracked her captor.

Silas's arms had silently twined around Colin's throat. His handsome face had distorted into sharp edges. His long fingers were losing their claw-like grip on Silas's hands.

Nat's lips thinned into a line, knowing the outcome. Colin's elegance would be no match for Silas's scrappiness. She sank against Jesse's chest.

Colin slipped to the ground, unconscious. Silas lowered himself, not letting up on the choke hold.

Jesse called out with authority. "Hands off, Sy. He needs to answer for his crimes."

Silas backed off. Granted, he acted rather snarly about it.

As she moved toward him, Jesse gripped her hands. "Not now, Nat. Let him decompress."

Oh. Understanding broke through her cloudy thinking. Slowly, she took stock of her surroundings.

A crowd had gathered. Silas tied the thug's hands behind his back with a cord from a pocket. Colin still lay in a heap on the ground. Judging from Silas's fierce countenance, Nat had no doubt Colin would be next. Jesse whispered something in her ear, then steered her toward his Jeep. Her short-lived adrenaline surge had vanished. After a shower, she wanted to sleep for days.

The blessed sound of sirens hurrying toward them pierced the atmosphere. Nat blissfully inhaled the salty air.

Silas waited at a corner table at a classic Mexican restaurant, hoping Nat would approve. He'd glanced over the menu. It had a decent a la carte selection—surely, she'd find something halfway nutritious. Most importantly, she'd agreed to come. It'd been a day and a half since the race, but he'd had no closure. He needed to know—had he sealed his fate when he took Colin down? Was this the end, or possibly a new beginning? He knew which one he wanted.

After they gave statements to the police, Jesse took Nat to the ER. Silas hustled to the hospital to check on Gramps.

Lacy had lied about several things, yet she'd told the truth about Gramps—even if she'd exaggerated the danger. Gramps had been so caught up in the race, he hadn't paid enough attention to the triple digit heat. Dehydration had taken its toll. Once they hooked him up to an IV, in short order, he grew ornery as ever, aggravated he'd missed the ultimate moments of their race.

He'd texted Nat to let her know Gramps would be fine. He pressed about her doctor's visit, but she'd brushed it off as no big deal. It stymied him. For cryin' out loud, they'd spent three days and nights in a boat together. She ought to know she could tell him anything.

Her lack of communication ate at him. Either she didn't remember that fantastic kiss or decided it was the worst mistake ever. Silas didn't care for either option. He missed her. Her cheery outlook on life brought hope to his weary soul. With her by his side, his future looked bright. He couldn't imagine working at Peeps without her. No way he would go back to his dreary routine. She made life fun again. He'd rarely found much reason to talk ... until Nat. All those hours alone in the boat had bonded them in ways he couldn't comprehend. Nor did he want to. He simply wanted to enjoy her presence.

His old self would let whatever they had wither and die from lack of attention. However, he'd discovered a new determination not to crawl back into his cave of isolation. No way he would let this go. What they shared had been exceptional.

So here he sat, trying not to fret. The server had already stopped by twice. His icy glass of tea soothed his sweaty palms. He checked his phone. Running late, of course. She hadn't texted either. Neither good news nor bad. He'd offered to pick her up, but she would only agree to meet him here. Another strike against him. How many strikes did he have left?

Before that miserable thought took hold, he spied her and bid his heart goodbye. Decked out in a flashy red blouse and jeans, she wore her hair down. The dark tresses tumbled over her shoulders, bouncing his pulse higher than the choppy bay waters.

NAT SPOTTED Silas in a corner booth and hurried over to meet him. "Sorry I'm late—" The flow of words stopped once he stood. Oh, goodness. This Silas wore clean pressed jeans and a lightweight plaid hoodie that complimented his deep hazel eyes. "Do I know you? I'm looking for a grubby guy in shorts," spilled out before she could catch it.

A glint of something shone in his eyes. "Grubby guy stayed home. You'll just have to keep up with me."

She laughed, feeling much more at ease. "I'm so glad to see you. We never got to—"

"We'll do it tonight. Our belated celebration." He took her hand, helped her into the booth, then slid in next to her.

Her heart fluttered at his gaze. Eyes and mouth soft, no hard lines in his face. No exhaustion. Or exasperation. Genuinely glad to see her too. Her stomach flipped.

Once the server had taken their drink orders, Silas asked, "What did the doctor say about your ... injuries?"

"Well, Jesse had a right to be concerned." She was still working through the guilt at the way she'd treated him. "The main culprit is a bruised rib. Turns out, sitting up for most of the race helped to alleviate the pain, though you could have fooled me. And the doctor didn't care for the nonstop part. My road to recovery includes rest. I'm supposed to lay off strenuous activities. Antibiotics for infection, though I hate them with a passion. 'Please don't re-injure the rib, Miss Jacobs. No canoe racing for a few months,'" she finished in a playfully authoritative tone. Any excuse not to paddle for a few weeks suited her fine.

"I'm gonna make sure of it."

"Sounds as if you know me, partner." Nat grinned, taking a sip of her lemon water.

"Like you know me." Silas's echo made her skin prickle. If only.

They ordered food, but Nat didn't remember what she ate. Well, aside from some bites from Silas's plate. She didn't know what to think of their food-sharing habit, except when it came from Silas, she'd liked almost anything. Mostly, she feasted on the man who sat next to her.

"What about the guy with the red cap who showed us the way out?" she mused. "Do you think he was real? We couldn't both have imagined him."

"Real as you and me sitting here. Yet ... not of this world." Silas gave her a knowing look.

Nat agreed. "Yeah, his timing was ... supernatural, I think. We were both about to throw in the towel."

"The way he disappeared when we recognized where we were. As if he knew the exact nanosecond we'd be okay." Silas rubbed a hand over his freshly shaven jaw.

She took a sip from her glass of tea. What a mystery. Yet she remained perfectly content with her lack of comprehension. "Tell me what happened after Lacy told you about Gramps. How did you know it was a trap?"

"I didn't. They were counting on me being single-minded about getting to Gramps. Except I was already missing you. When I looked back, I saw Lacy holding a gun. Thank goodness Jesse showed up." Silas's eyes widened. "I had gone into sniper mode, getting ready to shoot someone. I hope he doesn't hold it against me."

She could speak to that. "Nah. Jess, of all people, understands what it is to get caught up in the moment. He's fought with Colin too."

"It's true, then." Silas's eyes lit with curiosity. "They fought about you?"

Nat lifted a shoulder. "What can I say? The men in my life get protective."

They sat in companionable silence while the server cleared

their table. By tacit agreement, they chose not to discuss the less pleasant parts of that day. Her name-calling. His intent to silence Colin—forever. All still too fresh.

Silas cleared his throat. "Nat, I'm sorry for the trouble Lacy caused. It's funny how you don't really know a person until—" He searched for the right way to say it.

"You've been in a boat with them for three days and nights?" Nat supplied.

His eyes crinkled at the corners. "Yeah."

"How did Lacy get involved with Colin, anyway?" She'd hot-footed it away from the scene, but the police found her in a matter of hours.

"I met her at Peeps. She knew Colin because she had dated his bodyguard-slash-thug. Colin used her connection with me to get information about you and the race. He'd been biding his time, waiting for the right opportunity to, um, reclaim your affections."

"He wanted me for a pet," Nat retorted. "What will happen to Lacy now? Seems to me she just fell in with the wrong crowd. Colin influenced her dislike of me, but that in itself doesn't make her a hardened criminal."

"She's not. Tavo said it will work in her favor. She's looking for a deal, singing like a canary about the role Colin played. Her testimony is what they need to put him away." Silas fiddled with a spoon, then laid it on the table. "Can't say I'm sorry."

A sigh escaped Nat's lips. "I wish Colin had made different choices. However much I may want to, I can't change someone. Only God can do that. Even then, the person has to want it."

Silas's thick brows scrunched. "Did you love him?"

Nat shook her head, wistfully noting how the lines in his forehead smoothed. "More like a brief infatuation. At first, I enjoyed going to fancy restaurants and doing things, well, the expensive way." Her shoulders lifted, then dropped. "It wore thin after a while." Silas's dark eyes probed, but he said nothing. Sheesh. The man talked little but communicated volumes.

"Colin was secretive. I rarely saw the person behind the mask. Once I did, it scared me. So, to answer your question, no, he didn't make my heart go pitter-pat." As she said it, a weight lifted off her chest.

Another item clamored for attention. Hazy recollections of Silas holding her around a small campfire plagued her. Easy enough to figure how they got there, given the level of their closeness during those last trying hours. Something else tickled at the back of her mind, but nothing surfaced. "What happened at the makeshift fishing camp?"

CHAPTER TWENTY-SEVEN

"You don't remember?" He gazed at her until she wanted to squirm.

"Not a clue." Foggy recollections didn't count. She couldn't dredge up any scrap of a memory. It bothered her more than she wanted to say.

"Are we done here? We need to take a walk." He signaled the server for their ticket.

Nat grew increasingly agitated as they squabbled over the bill. Silas insisted on paying, even though it wasn't a date. Was it? She gave in with the stipulation she would pay next time. Hopeful assumption on her part, especially if she'd thrown herself at him at the fish camp. Would he tell her the truth? Could she bear to hear it?

Before they left the restaurant, she ducked into the ladies' room. Silas held her helmet, seeming in no hurry. Was that a good sign? Her heart beat in triple time. What if he planned to let her down easy?

MINUTE PINK BLOSSOMS covered the sidewalk. The overarching crepe myrtle trees reminded her of the tree canopies on the rivers. "I enjoyed the event, even if I'm not ready to get in another canoe for a while. With or without bruises," she added the last part with a wry smile.

He turned to her. "Paddling with you is one of my favorite things, Nat." His eyes flickered with an emotion she couldn't read. "You really don't remember?"

Oh, no. She'd acted so inappropriately he'd chosen to keep her at the opposite end of the boat. Again. "Please tell me I did nothing to regret." Dread whispered the words.

He leaned closer. Uh-oh. His lips stopped an inch from hers. "What if I said we kissed?"

Her breath came out in a sharp hiss. "Is that what happened?"

"Yes. A fisherman interrupted us." His mouth moved to her ear. His whisper had her insides quivering. "I'd love to finish what we started—if it's what you want."

Bits and pieces rushed back. A guy hollering at them. The sun-bleached tarp. Ashy chips of charcoal in the sand. Her side aching abominably. "You wanted to build a house."

"With you."

"What does that mean?"

"It means I love you, Nat." He dropped a kiss on her neck on the way back to her mouth.

Nat tilted her head back and let his lips claim hers. She sank into his embrace, happy to let him be in charge. Until she had no air. Pulling away with reluctance, she caught her breath.

She searched his face. "You're serious?"

His eyes darkened with desire. "Never been more serious about anything. Do you want me?"

She nodded slowly. "I've always wanted you. We landed in a boat race because I couldn't leave you alone."

"I'm glad you didn't." His raspy voice blanketed her. He'd snugged his arms around her waist, making her feel secure.

"Not at first," Nat teased.

"No," he admitted, tightening his hold the teensiest bit. "Except during the race, I got to know the woman behind the pretty face. And now I'm crazy about you." He claimed her lips in another kiss.

They slowly broke apart. Nat tamed his thick brows with her thumb, then tucked loose strands of hair behind his ear. "Um. Delicious. Much better than a sugary dessert."

Silas's newly smoothed brows raised. "For once, I agree." His molten gaze curled her toes. "And you know how fond I am of second helpings." He brushed his lips over hers.

As she smiled against his lips, he kissed her again. And again. Until she lost count because of the delightful way he was exploring her mouth.

Finally, he leaned his forehead against hers with a slight groan. "Does this have to stop? I've wanted to kiss you for so long, it's not near enough."

His words warmed her to the core, but she couldn't resist teasing him. "Hm. When did 'so long' happen?"

A tender smile played about his lips. "It started way back when you gave me the cowboy hat. We were still arguing a lot, so I ignored the idea. But your can-do attitude during the race with one catastrophe after another—you never gave up even when everything we'd worked for seemed lost. That's when I knew ... you were all I wanted."

His eyes hardened. "Once I realized Colin had you—"

"Shh ... I'm fine." She kissed his tight jaw, pleased when the tenseness in his body ebbed.

He nuzzled her neck, whispering, "You *are* fine."

Oh, gracious. Any more sweet talk and she'd melt into a puddle of goo all over the sidewalk. Her phone buzzed. Probably Jesse. His overprotectiveness still tried her patience, but she was working to change her thinking. He checked on her because he cared. That, in itself, was a gift. An idea sparked through her lovely haze.

She leaned into Silas, choosing her words. "As tempting as it is to stay here and kiss you, Jesse promised to show me the rehab plans tonight. Why don't you come with me since it concerns you too? Besides, he needs to get used to the idea of *us*."

"Oh, he's already aware of *us*. He's just not a fan of *me*," Silas said dryly.

Nat tossed her head. "He goes overboard about the men in my life. Nobody's good enough, yada, yada." She gave him a smug look. "I know better than anyone. If Jesse didn't trust you, he wouldn't have proposed we do the 'toughest canoe race in the world' together."

"So we're back in their good graces? Jesse and Mr. Spence?"

"Yeppers. They want the whole thing behind us ASAP. Mostly they don't want any reporters sniffing around Peeps. It's still hard to believe Colin would confront me in broad daylight. Talk about stupid. I mean, there were people around, even if they weren't close by."

Silas steered her chin to his face, his other hand nestling into the small of her back. "Tavo asked me—no, he cornered me—at the gym for my version of what happened. Once I told him, he said you must have been Colin's Achilles heel. The police have been trying to pin him for years, and he's always eluded them. His downfall was coming after you."

Nat snorted. "His arrogance caused it. He doesn't believe the law applies to him. Enough about Colin though." She inched forward. "I'd rather be in a canoe with you any day."

Silas closed the gap, kissing her on the nose. His throat rumbled. "All other places, too, if I get a vote. You taste like hope. I need hope—I need *you* by my side." He kissed her again. "I want our new beginning." Slowly, he released her. Retrieving her helmet from the bench, he handed it to her.

Sighing, she put the helmet on. A shower of sparkle dust sprinkled down her face. Confused, she stared at it, then took off the helmet. Glitter shimmered—in her hair, down the front of her blouse, on her hands—she stared at him, comprehending by degrees.

His lips twitched with mischief. "Gotcha, Glitter Girl."

She nuzzled her head into the front of his shirt, then held on to him. "I got you too, Grouch."

His endearing half-smirk appeared. "You do." His lips met hers again. A soft sigh escaped as she leaned into his solid chest. Jesse would understand.

Kissing the Grouch had become her new priority.

AUTHOR'S NOTE

Dear Readers,

I so enjoyed writing *Glitter and the Grouch*! Well, aside from a few head-banging sessions to make sure the canoe race happened in a realistic manner.

I've always been fascinated by the Texas Water Safari, so it's a joy to give back in a small way. If my story has piqued your interest, just go to the website, https://www. texaswatersafari.org/. There you'll find all-things TWS. During the actual race, it's possible to track the progress of each entry online. YouTube also has many videos of the different races which helped me to understand the rigorous nature of the event.

Nat and Silas are the two secondary characters from books 1 & 2 who became quite insistent about having their story told. Their love story was fun to write. Despite Silas's taciturn ways, he managed to surprise me several times, and Nat's impulsiveness kept me guessing as to what she'd do next.

If you loved this story and haven't read books 1 and 2, you may want to go back for the rest of the Valiant saga. Jesse and

Brenna experience quite the rollercoaster ride in *Countin' On Jesse,* and Rory and Vi's story in *Lovin' On Red* is, by turns, prickly and tender. Stay tuned for book 4, *Waitin' on Paige,* where Paige and Tavo have their chance at love—if either of them can slow down long enough to make it happen.

As always, if you enjoyed this book, please take a few minutes to post a review, especially on Amazon, then Goodreads and Bookbub. It doesn't have to be long. A star rating and two or three sentences telling what you loved about the story is an enormous help.

Thank you for reading my stories. I hope your reading experience is fun, uplifting, and your takeaway is a smile.

Blessings,

Mary Pat

ACKNOWLEDGMENTS

I've always had a keen interest in the Texas Water Safari, the annual canoe race that takes place every spring in Texas. The length of the race is 260 miles. That's a very long distance in a small boat. The notorious Texas heat also makes a difference. Any given year, low water due to lack of rainfall can change difficult conditions to downright dangerous.

The critters and varmints that inhabit Texas rivers, i.e., poisonous snakes, bugs, spiders, and mosquitoes, make it tough as well. The sheer number of times a boat needs portaging takes a tremendous physical toll. The term "hallucination alley" is genuine, used to describe both the physical and mental deterioration that happens when a boater has been awake an extended length of time. This race earned the moniker "the toughest canoe race in the world."

Some competitors have no interest in winning the race. Under such harsh conditions, they consider completing the race to be a win all in itself. But for those who care about the rankings, the DNF (did not finish) label is far worse than coming in last.

That said, there's something about the Texas Water Safari that gets in a person's blood. I had the privilege of interviewing Bill Stafford, a longtime competitor in the race. He has raced it thirty-one times and is competing again this year. When I mentioned that I wanted to write a story about the TWS, he scratched his head but politely answered everything I asked.

Later, I told him it turned out as a love story, and the TWS was the vehicle through which it happened, he smiled and said that very scenario had cropped up more than once through the years. His book, *The Texas Water Safari Has A Polecat In It*, proved a huge blessing to my research efforts in making the story accurate. Any mistakes are mine alone.

K.C. Boren and his wife, Charley, were also indispensable to my research. Charley had a scrapbook with pictures that I pored over many times to glean race details. K.C. had drawn a map on the inside of his boat that inspired a similar incident in my story.

The TWS is a safe, family-oriented race. The suspense scenes in my story are pure fiction. Those type of things have NEVER happened in all the years of the race.

I'd also like to acknowledge Kerry Henneke, P.T. and owner of Alliant Rehabilitation and Sports Therapy in Victoria, Texas. He was my inspiration for Silas, the main character in my story. Kerry is tough, but after my hip surgery, he knew "how to fix the hitch in my git-along." And Cathy Verduzco, a personal trainer at Citizen's HealthPlex, helped me model Nat's job as a PT.

No book ever writes itself. It takes other people to make it the best it can be. Many thanks to Linda Fulkerson, the owner of Scrivenings Press. Her vision for publishing helped make my dream come true. And her book cover skills are the best. Kudos to Regina Merrick, my content editor, and Heidi Glick, my line editor. You gals make my work shine.

As always, I couldn't write without the support of my family. Mom, who always wants me to hurry up and finish the next one so she can read it, and my adult children, Nancy and Phillip. You guys always have my back. And to Dave...your insights and steady stream of patience keep me going. Hope you see yourself in Silas...every hero I create has a facet of your character.

And to Jesus Christ, my Lord. Thank you for your faithfulness to help me write this story. From the Holy-Spirit-whispers in my ear, the surprises, and the daily ups and downs of writing, you were always there.

ABOUT THE AUTHOR

Mary Pat Johns' writing career began once she retired from teaching speech and writing. She's written devotions for an online publication and has short stories published by *Chicken Soup for the Soul*. She currently writes a weekly faith column for her local newspaper.

Countin' On Jesse, her first novel, debuted in 2023, and book 2 of the Valiant series, *Lovin' On Red*, released in April 2024. God put it in her heart to tell stories of brave veterans and their reintegration into civilian life after suffering the traumas of war. Later, it expanded to include anyone who had survived difficult circumstances.

Her writing often focuses on flawed characters who encounter the extravagant grace of God. At this time, she's busily at work completing the fourth and last novel of the Valiant series and planning her next series.

She lives in South Texas with her husband and their two dapple dachshunds. Her grown children and five grandchildren are useful sorts, who keep her grounded with her reading/writing obsession. You can find her at the gym, at her computer, or reading a good book.

ALSO BY MARY PAT JOHNS

Romance in Valiant—Book One

Accountant Brenna McKinley only wants what's best for Peeps, the wildly popular gym in Valiant, Texas. But when money goes missing, and she's the obvious suspect, will she be able to clear her name or face criminal charges? Keeping her dream job matters, but falling in love with her boss isn't part of the plan. Neither is the creepy guy stalking her.

Young veteran Jesse Jacobs manages and co-owns Peeps. He needs help to gain accreditation for the exercise facility, and his new accountant is all in. But is she who she seems? Too bad he's falling for her like a man with no parachute. When the pressure builds, PTSD renders him moody and volatile, risking everything he loves.

Get your copy here:

https://scrivenings.link/countinonjesse

Romance in Valiant—Book Two

Rory is a wildly successful contractor with all the right connections. He has everything, except the woman who sees past his missing foot. If only the tiny redhead he's insanely attracted to would go on a date with him, it could work, but Vi refuses.

Licensed massage therapist Vi Summers needs her childhood home remodeled, and Rory Spence is the perfect man for the job. Only he's the last person she wants to work with. Despite Rory's reputation as a flirt, his tender attention to getting her house right helps Vi see into his heart. Too bad her past mistakes prevent a future relationship.

Drawn together like magnets, they navigate trouble with illegal squatters, family expectations, and fire. Will they finally be honest with each other, or will their secrets tear them apart?Get your copy here:

https://scrivenings.link/lovinonred

Stay up-to-date on your favorite books and authors with our free e-newsletters.

ScriveningsPress.com